DAVID
AT
OLIVET

DAVID AT OLIVET

Wallace Hamilton

St. Martin's Press · New York

Library of Congress Cataloging in Publication Data

Hamilton, Wallace, 1919–
    David at Olivet.

    1. David, King of Israel—Fiction.   2. Jonathan, son of Saul—Fiction. I. Title.
PZ4.H2212Dav [PS3558.A4443]   813'.5'4   78-19437
ISBN 0-312-18366-6
ISBN 0-312-18367-4 pbk.

For my
third-born son

ONE

D avid, King of Israel and Judah, walked the dusty path
up Mount Olivet barefoot. He wore a robe of rough
linen; his head was uncovered and the sun was hot on his
forehead. Pebbles hurt his feet and he was beginning to
feel fingers of pain etching lines on his back. He kept walking, with the measured gait of a man who has marched most
of his life.

Behind walked the members of the King's household,
weeping soft sobs that seemed to melt in the wind and
eddy around the rhythmic clanking of soldiers in armor.
When the path turned, David paused to look back, far
down the gorge of Kidron to Jerusalem on the crest of Zion.
Deep in the valley, the slow-moving priests and Levites
were carrying the Ark of the Covenant back to Jerusalem.
On his orders.

The Ark would not follow the King, but would stay in
Jerusalem. As would the loyal high priests, Zadok and Abiathar. Of Zadok he had asked, "Can you make use of your
eyes?" Zadok assured him his eyes saw, and his ears heard.
They understood each other.

Had Absalom and his troops entered Jerusalem? David's
decision to abandon the city to his son had been made at

1

daybreak that morning. Joab, his commanding general, had led him to a lookout on the city wall; across the valley on the western hill he could see the massing of Israelite troops, the dust rising from their movements, the faint shouts of orders floating across the morning air.

Joab's voice was insistent, close to his ear. "We took Jerusalem from the Jebusites, David. Absalom can take it from us. This place will be our prison, and our coffin. We've got to get out, into the open, where we can move, and counterattack. Let Jerusalem be *their* coffin."

A coffin for Absalom? His son? But he gave the order to leave.

Now, on the slope of Olivet, David wondered. *If I had walked out the city gates in the early morning sun, barefoot, sought out Absalom among his troops, embraced him with fatherly warmth?* He suspected that one stroke of an Israelite sword would have ended his reign. *Would it have mattered? One tired head separated from one tired body? Would that have mattered?* He could imagine passing into Sheol, far in the west across the Great Sea, and there he would find . . . Yes, he would find Jonathan.

The pain in his back suddenly wrenched him back to the present. He gasped for breath, stumbled, and sat down on a rock beside the path. Bathsheba hurried up to him and put her hand on his shoulder. "What is wrong, my Lord?"

"My back. It will pass."

"Do you want a litter?"

David straightened and the pain stabbed again. Between breaths: "I . . . will . . . walk."

"Rest for a moment." Bathsheba sat beside him, their son Solomon pressing close to her.

David heard the commands, ringing down the path, *halt for the King!* He felt powerless; the pain in his back could stop a small army. He felt poured out like water, all his bones out of joint, and his strength dried up like a potsherd.

2

He had written so, once, in a fit of depression, and now all the dark dreams of his song seemed to be coming true.

He looked around. "Where is Ira?"

David's personal priest, a young man with a quizzical expression, appeared before him and bowed. "My Lord, can I help you?"

"Only God can help me." David pressed his hand against his lower spine. "But you can sympathize."

"Are you ill?" And he came forward with a gentle movement.

David sighed. "In addition to my beloved son Absalom, and several armies from the northern tribes and Judah . . . not to mention the Philistines, Amalekites, Edomites, Moabites, and the wild bull of Bashan . . . now my back."

"You have been afflicted before. And it passed."

"I *know* . . ." he gasped again in pain, ". . . it will pass. But it occurs to me, Ira, that considering my back, the old wound in my shoulder, the miseries of my right knee, and the head pains I get whenever the prophet Nathan assails me with some truth . . . considering all these things, Ira, I think I need a completely new body."

Ira grinned faintly. "Each of us is given just one."

"Easy enough for the likes of you to say. That young body of yours works. It is said that Methuselah lived nine hundred and sixty-nine years. Is it too much for God to allow me to live fifty-six—one more year, at least?" And David tried to look deeply hurt.

Ira knew the game. As priest, as sacrificial goat, he was to take the blame for all David's frustrations and displeasures. His sacrifices failed to appease; his supplications went unheeded; his divine protection had fallen like a cloak—and Ira was to blame.

Ira's defense was to mouth the most fatuous of priestly wisdom, knowing David wasn't fooled. It was their game, a game David could not play with any other priest or Levite. Ira raised his eyes to heaven. "God will bless you. Have faith."

David beckoned to Ira. "Come closer."

Ira bowed his head.

David whispered. "Could it be, Ira, that God doesn't like me much, anymore?"

Ira whispered back. "Do you really need God if you have Joab?"

David looked at Ira, scandalized.

But Ira was unfazed. "I think it is probable, however, that you will have the strength of both."

The trace of a smile broke briefly on David's face; then his eyes grew serious. Ira responded with a look as serious, putting his hand on the King's shoulder, and David covered it with his own for just a moment. But the game was resumed. David said, in a mimic of priestly tones, "Yes, we shall have faith."

"Indeed, my Lord, indeed."

Joab came clanking up through the King's retinue and stood before David, frowning. "Your back, again?"

David was rueful. "Yes, Joab."

"Damnit! We can't have this delay." He stared at David sharply. "I'll have you carried."

"I . . . will . . . not . . . be carried."

"Stubborn! What are we supposed to do? Wait here until Absalom and his rag-tail troops come to cut us down? They can, you know. While you nurse your stubborn pride!"

David glared at Joab. "I . . . will . . . walk . . . up Olivet."

Joab tugged at his beard furiously. "Can you stand?"

"I can try."

Joab held out an arm, ridged with cords of muscle and bound by a studded leather thong. "Here. Hold on."

David reached and held Joab's arm with both his hands. "Ready?"

David tightened his lips and nodded. As Joab raised his

4

arm, David came to his feet quivering with pain and stood there, breathing hard.

"Ira," Joab barked. "Take the other side."

Ira came forward quickly.

David, a warrior to one side and a priest to the other, continued to climb Mount Olivet. His steps were slow and pain hardened his face. But he climbed, and climbing, thought about Absalom.

He knew what his counselors thought. His son was so petulant, so vain, so headstrong, that he would never be able to hold together the fragile union of Judah and the northern tribes of Israel. That unity had been one of the triumphs of David's statecraft—a delicate political refinement of Saul's magnetic leadership, which had brought all the tribes of Jacob together for the first time since their arrival in Canaan. With Absalom, what would happen? Would the tribes slip back into the anarchy of the time of the Judges, to be picked off, one by one, by the enemies surrounding them? It wasn't simply a matter of Absalom; it was a matter of the survival of the tribes of Jacob. David's counselors feared Absalom as a mortal threat.

David himself was not so sure. The fact that, at twenty-five, Absalom had been able to organize a revolt strong enough to force David to leave Jerusalem was evidence of impressive leadership. And he would mature. But how? He had beauty, presence, and command, as David had had when he became king of Judah at thirty. He had heritage, not only through David; through his mother he was related to the royalty of the northern tribes. If he was vain, he had an intelligence to be vain about.

Why were his counselors so set against Absalom? Oh, yes, loyalty to David—and their own good fortunes in the royal court. That was evident. But in moments of depression, David had let it be known he might abdicate and let power pass peacefully to Absalom. How Hushai had opposed it, fire in his eye! And Zadok and Abiathar. Only Ahithophel wavered. Now Ahithophel had gone over to Absalom. All the others stayed with David. Why? What was this fear of Absalom?

And what was the fear inside himself? Why was it that he could look down on Jerusalem from Olivet and fear for its people, knowing Absalom was coming? Something about his eyes. He had noticed them ever since Absalom had grown to adolescence, an adolescent of extraordinary grace, body lithe and molded, lustrous dark hair flowing to his shoulders, facial features of exotic, almost Egyptian regularity. But his eyes seemed to turn inward, as if they were mirrors for him to see his own beauty. They rested like still pools. Only sometimes did they look outward, but when they did, it was with the focus of some predatory bird. Then that focused vision blazed with an intensity that seemed to promise a plummeting swoop, an animal cry, and blood.

David had known the spilling of blood ever since he had come to Saul's court. Sometimes, in the fury of battle, he had spilled it wantonly. But he had never seen such a look in a man's eyes as he saw in Absalom's.

For years it had been the custom in Jerusalem at the royal house—the House of Cedar—to have the household gather after evening meal. David would play his harp and the young people of the court would take turns dancing before the King. Sometimes it was Amnon. Sometimes Tamar. Or Absalom. Or even a young concubine gifted with suppleness of movement. All except Mephibosheth, Jonathan's son, a cripple since childhood. He sat beside the King, following the rhythm of the music with finger cymbals.

Absalom vied with the others for a time to dance . . . before the King, before the court, before an audience whose

6

gaze would caress the beauty of his person. Once he had gathered all the visions to himself, there in the center of the room, he would drape them about his body like silk and move in the folds with sightless languor, his hands stroking his body to the flow of the music. All eyes upon him, he seemed to rejoice in his sheathed solitude.

One evening the eyes turned outward and fixed upon Mephibosheth, sitting with his shoulder resting on David's knee. In turn after turn of the dance, Absalom's eyes came back to Mephibosheth's broken body. Finally, with a toss of his head, Absalom stood still, his eyes unblinking, a smile on his lips. "There now, it is enough for me. It is Mephibosheth's turn to dance."

People in the room gasped. Mephibosheth looked startled; then he stared at the floor, his shoulders hunched as if to ward off Absalom's voice.

But the voice was insistent. "Come, to your feet, Mephibosheth! Show the King how you dance." He prowled toward the sitting figure. "What's the matter? Can't you stand? What are you? Just a cripple? And you think you are fit for a king's court?"

David's voice crackled. "Absalom, leave my sight!"

With a twist of his body, a smile still on his lips, Absalom left, walking in triumph.

That was ten years ago, or more. David had been warned, had he read the signs. But he hoped Absalom would change, that the cruelty would fade in time. When he had thought about it. But a king has many things to think about.

Still, even now he saw how Mephibosheth had looked at him when Absalom had left—and his eyes were the eyes of Jonathan, and his brow was the brow of Jonathan, and his lips were the lips of Jonathan—and he had said, "I would dance for you, my Lord."

David had put his hand on Mephibosheth's shoulder to keep him seated. "But the music needs the cymbals."

7

For twenty-five years, David had lived with the ache of the loss of Jonathan, killed along with Saul in battle with the Philistines at Gilboa. The cry in his heart had become a poem, and when the grief of memory became too great, he would dismiss everyone, take up his harp, and sing, as if to call Jonathan back from Sheol.

How are the mighty fallen in the midst of the battle!
O Jonathan, thou wast slain in thine high places.
I am distressed for thee, my brother Jonathan:
very pleasant hast thou been unto me:
thy love for me was wonderful, passing the love of women.
How are the mighty fallen,
and the weapons of war perished!

Once King of Israel as well as Judah, and having established the royal city at Jerusalem, David began to feel the loneliness of rule, and images of Jonathan grew more vivid in his mind. The shapes and forms of his body. The ease of his grin. The sound of his voice and the touch of his hand. Memories so clear and insistent that sometimes, half-waking at night, he could feel Jonathan beside him, and all else sloughed away.

Nothing left. No sword or garment. No thong or lock of hair.

It had been so long . . . the exile from Saul's court, and then the disaster at Gilboa. What had happened to Jonathan while David was in exile?

David had spoken to Hushai. "Do we know of any member of Saul's family that I could care for, for Jonathan's sake?"

Hushai said he would make inquiries.

Several days later Hushai reappeared at David's court, bringing with him a fussy little man with a scraggly beard and protruding lower lip. His name was Ziba, and he bowed so low before the King that David feared he might fall on his face.

"You have information about Saul's family?"

Ziba's voice was hasty with nervousness. "Yes, my Lord, yes . . . yes . . ."

"Well?"

"But . . . but . . . but . . . my master, he fears you."

"Who is your master?"

"Mephibosheth, son of Jonathan, son of Saul."

David felt his heart quicken. He had found flesh of Jonathan's flesh.

"Why should Mephibosheth fear me?"

"He is the seed of Saul. It might be said that he was a threat to your throne." Ziba raised a quivering hand. "But . . . but . . . he is no threat. He is lame in both legs and it is difficult for him even to walk, let alone command an army."

David felt a glow of protective warmth. "Bring Mephibosheth to me."

"Yes, my Lord . . . yes, as you command . . ." He bowed low again, saliva glistening on his lower lip, and kept bowing until he was out of the room.

David turned to Hushai. "A strange man, that Ziba."

"I would not trust him."

David shrugged. "Still, he will bring me the son of Jonathan."

Hushai's quiet eyes looked at David thoughtfully. "It is still strong with you, isn't it, the memory of Jonathan?"

"As strong as any I have."

"What was it about him?"

David was silent for a moment. "When I was with him, I felt as if I were high at Shiloh, swept by great winds and warmed in blazing sunlight. For a time, I lived through him, and it has never been the same."

"Perhaps . . ." Hushai stared into space, ". . . a time like that is your special blessing."

When Mephibosheth entered the royal audience chamber, accompanied by Ziba, David thought he was seeing a ghost. There before him was the image of Jonathan as a youth, the high brow, the shock of dark hair, and the set of the shoulders. David held himself from moving, from crossing the room to embrace him. And then the figure moved . . .

He moved with a slow grotesque hobble, his hand resting on Ziba's shoulder for support. His eyes were downcast, checking each painful step, until he came before the King. Then his eyes lifted to look at David like some wounded animal.

Mephibosheth bowed low. David noticed that he trembled as he did so.

"Mephibosheth . . ."

"Your servant, my Lord."

". . . do not be afraid."

Mephibosheth raised his head and looked at David questioningly.

David spoke low, as if to calm a tethered goat. "I mean to show you kindness for your father's sake. I will give you back the whole estate of your grandfather Saul. You shall have a place for yourself at my table."

Mephibosheth's voice was choked. "Who am I that you should spare a thought for me?"

David stretched out a hand and touched Mephibosheth's trembling shoulder. "The sign of a pledge I made long ago." He wanted to take the boy in his arms. But he did not.

David turned to Ira, his back laced with stabbing pains.

"Ira. Where is Mephibosheth? We left the city in great haste. Was he left behind?"

"Yes, my Lord, I believe so."

David fretted. He remembered the look in Absalom's eyes and Absalom would be entering Jerusalem. What would he do to a grandson of Saul? He turned to Joab. "If Mephibosheth is in the city, we ought to rescue him."

10

Joab stared at David. "And have some men taken captive in the process, carrying him like baggage?" Joab snorted. "We have enough baggage. He's better off where he is."

"I do not know what Absalom will do with him."

"David, come to your senses! It is enough that we rescue the kingdom from that mad son of yours."

David nodded, and continued to climb Olivet. The pebbles seemed sharper under his bare feet.

TWO

Mephibosheth stood at his window in the House of Cedar, looking over the gorge of Kidron, and watched the priests slowly carrying the Ark of the Covenant back to Jerusalem. The afternoon sun splashed golden on the hills across the gorge, but the gorge itself was deep in purple shadow; the movement of the priests seemed ominous, as if they brought David's spirit back to its final resting place in the Tabernacle.

Yet David was alive. Far up the gorge, a cloud of dust on the side of Olivet and an occasional flash of metal proved that the King was there with his troops. But in flight. And the Ark was being returned. Would he ever see David again? He felt his life draining away.

The royal court had been in an uproar that morning, once David had given the order to leave. The shouts. The bustle of slaves. The tramp of the marching Royal Guards through the corridors. The massing of troops in the courtyard outside the house. Mephibosheth had tried to get to David in the audience room, but Joab had turned him back. The guards had carelessly pushed him against the wall, time and again, as they marched in and out. He limped along trying to find his aunt, Michal, who might help get an ass or litter to carry him . . . to follow David. But he could not find her in the confusion. And where was his servant Ziba?

He went back to his chambers, falling once and having his foot stepped on when one of the guards could not see him prone in the darkness of the corridor. The pain was excruciating and he had to crawl the last few paces back to his room. He had lain on his pallet, waiting and panting with pain. David would come for him. David would send a messenger. David would not leave him . . . not to wait for Absalom. No . . .

Then Ziba had come.

"An ass! A litter!" he had commanded. "I shall go too!"

But Ziba had held up that fidgety hand of his. "Be calm, now. Be calm. Yes . . . that is right . . . yes."

Mephibosheth, prone on the pallet, pointed to the door. "Do as I command!"

Ziba's lips were working. "In good time . . . yes . . . but . . ."

"Now!"

But Ziba had not moved. He just stood there, scratching his beard, and there was a strange look in his eye. "My Lord, we must think of the King . . ."

"I think of David! I want to be with him. I am of the King's court."

"But he is on a military campaign. He must be able to move swiftly, and . . . and . . ." Ziba had gestured at Mephibosheth's body and his voice had grown silken. "My Lord, if you love David, stay here and wait for him to win the victory."

"Victory? He has fled! I want to be with him in defeat."

"The King has retreated to gather his forces . . . he will return and strike." Ziba had shaken his head. "The King will not be defeated and will reward those who are loyal to him. Your loyalty is not to be a burden to him."

"A burden?" Mephibosheth looked Ziba in the eye and Ziba looked back, steadily, but still with that glint. Mephib-

13

osheth felt a flash of pain in his foot. "Burden . . ." He fell back on the pallet. "Go. Leave me."

Ziba had bowed and left the chambers, his sandals making a rustling sound on the cedar floor.

Mephibosheth stared at the dark wood of the ceiling. The shouting outside stabbed in his ears. He felt a hot welling of tears, and the sobs came hard.

Now, he looked at the cloud of dust on the golden mountain and imagined he marched beside David as Jonathan had marched, the slow, even strides ascending. They would fight Absalom as they had fought the Philistines, with swiftness and guile, striking out of nowhere to smite them in hip and thigh. He would be with David, as Jonathan had been with David in the power of the Lord, and in their love for each other.

So he dreamt. But there was the Ark, coming back to Jerusalem, the creeping figures in the shadows of Kidron, carrying it back, and David in flight. And Mephibosheth could barely hobble. He hated himself. He raged at his impotence. He cursed his broken legs and the waste of his life. Jonathan was the Sun. He was only shadow, dark as the gloom of his chambers.

He flung himself on the pallet and held his ears against the silence. David had left. Absalom would come. He was powerless.

Ziba had returned to Lo-debar from Jerusalem in a terrible fuss. Mephibosheth was sixteen then and living in seclusion at the house of Machir. With David on the throne, the grandson of Saul had no wish to draw attention to himself. As far as Mephibosheth was concerned, David's power was absolute; any rival could be crushed with one stroke of a paid sword.

But now Ziba came from Jerusalem. "The King wishes to see you, my Lord."

Mephibosheth felt the world closing in on him, all his fears suddenly realized. "For what reason?"

"He says . . ." Ziba paused significantly, ". . . he says he wants to show you kindness for Jonathan's sake."

"A trap?"

Ziba shrugged, his hands open to heaven. "I only report, my Lord, what the King said. I cannot tell you the secrets of his will."

Panic took hold of Mephibosheth. "I must flee. Philistia. Tyre. The deserts across the Jordan."

Ziba tugged at his robe with nervous fingers. "My Lord . . ."

"Prepare a caravan at once!"

"My Lord, a moment, please . . ."

"What would you have me do? Wait here for the King's assassins?"

"But perhaps you could have a larger life."

"What do you mean?"

"My Lord, you are the grandson of Saul. But you are also the son of Jonathan. The love of David and Jonathan is one of the legends of our time. It is possible that the King means what he says. If you find favor with the King, it will go well for all of us."

Mephibosheth stared at Ziba. "I know the legend. I think of it at night."

"It is day. Think of it now."

When the doors of the audience chamber opened, Mephibosheth looked into the eyes of the King, and there was a cry inside him for the home that he wanted. *I am flesh of the flesh you loved.* He held his eyes to the floor in front of him, so he would not falter or stumble. He would come to the King.

When he neared the throne, he raised his eyes again, and heard the voice of David, as soft as if it spoke to Jonathan, and he melted in the cadences of it. He felt caressed in sunlight warmth, and the King's touch on his shoulder calmed him. He would sit at King David's table.

In another part of the house, Michal, daughter of Saul, sister of Jonathan, wife of David, summoned a young male slave. "I want you to hasten to Ephraim. There you will find my lord, Paltiel, son of Laish. Tell him the King has fled Jerusalem, and I am alone here in the House of Cedar until Absalom comes. Tell him I have loved him and love him still. If he wishes me to return to his household, I will do so. I wait for him here. Now hurry!"

The slave bowed and left.

Michal paced the room. Perhaps her captivity was over. She had grown to detest David, and the thought of being reunited with Paltiel was sweet. In the years of their marriage she had grown to love him; she prayed he still loved her.

Her whole life had been ripped apart the day Abner, general to Saul and then to Saul's son, Ishbosheth, appeared at Paltiel's house in Ephraim, accompanied by some strutting guards. It was a quiet house because Paltiel was a quiet man. Their life together had flowed with the seasons—the planting of the grain, the shearing of the sheep, the harvesting of the figs. It had been her refuge from the clamor of Saul's court in Gibeah where she had spent her girlhood.

Now, with Abner, the clamor had returned to invade her home.

Abner was blunt. Abner was always blunt. "I come from your brother, Ishbosheth."

Michal was instantly wary, and she saw wariness reflected in Paltiel's watchful eyes. Jonathan had bestrode the ground; his younger brother Ishbosheth had always sidled over it. She wondered how he had managed to maintain the kingship of Israel. But with his weakness, he had wile . . . and he had Abner.

"What does Ishbosheth want in this place?"

Even Abner hesitated. "You, my lady."

16

Outside the wind whistled through the cedar trees around the house. Goats bleated. She could hear the talk of the slaves as they threshed grain.

"What does he want of me? I have my place here, with my husband."

"It is the will of your brother Ishbosheth, King of Israel, that you return to your husband, David, and become the queen of Judah. It is part of a state agreement between the two kings, and so insisted upon by David."

Michal's eyes blazed. "David is not . . . my husband. I was given to Paltiel by Saul, King of Israel and Judah, after David had fled the King's anger on our wedding night. We hardly knew each other as husband and wife, and after all these years he certainly is not . . . my husband! You violate Saul's will!"

Abner's voice was even and ominous. "I speak for two kings . . . who live."

"And scorn the memory of one greater than either of them! My father!"

Paltiel put his arm around his wife. "What Ishbosheth proposes is against law and tradition. You may return to Ishbosheth and tell him that. Or else he will be cursed of God."

Abner averted his eyes, but his voice was gruff. "It is not for me to tell the King anything. I follow orders. My lady is to come with me under guard, and I will escort her to Hebron."

"But David has no claim on her," Paltiel insisted. "She has been my faithful wife for years."

Abner shrugged and rattled his armor. "He paid two hundred Philistine foreskins for her and he wants her back."

Thus Michal was escorted to David in Hebron. Paltiel followed her as far as Bahurim, weeping all the way, until Abner ordered him back. Michal had not seen him since, and it had been years, but at the turn of each season she could picture to herself the life on Paltiel's fertile lands in Ephraim, and she ached to return.

It did not take long at Hebron for her to understand why

17

David had forced her to come to him as one of his several queens. The love they had had for each other at Gibeah—barely out of childhood—had long since vanished. Now she could look at him as a stranger, still beautiful to be sure, but intent, preoccupied, predatory, with a hawklike look that later she could see in Absalom. She knew the moment she laid eyes on David at Hebron that Ishbosheth was doomed, and she came to realize that her sole purpose in David's court was as daughter of Saul, the counter in David's court against Ishbosheth, son of Saul. She was there to pave the way for the killing of her brother and David's ascendancy to the throne of Israel. She was baggage to his statecraft.

Ishbosheth's death had not come as she had suspected. David could wear a cloak of innocence. But it had come, and she had seen the severed head of Ishbosheth brought to Hebron and witnessed with loathing David's pious outrage. She wondered how her brother Jonathan could have loved such a man.

Would Absalom now bring back the severed head of David to a triumph in Jerusalem? She thought of how the cycle of blood repeated itself, all in the name of God's anointment, and she wearied of it. She remembered one evening after nightfall in Ephraim. Not finding Paltiel in the house, she had gone, lamp in hand, to the cattle shed. There she had found him, sitting on the straw, feeding milk out of a bowl to a sick calf, nurturing it to life. She prayed that Paltiel would come for her and give her back her own life.

In the meantime she waited in her rooms in the nearly empty House of Cedar. It might be hours or days before she left and she would never see it again. She would not regret it. Then she thought of the one person in the court that she would miss: her nephew, Mephibosheth. Had he gone with David, or had David left him behind?

Leaving word with her maidservant, she walked down the echoing corridors to Mephibosheth's room. She found him in the dimness, lying on his pallet, his face flushed with cry-

18

ing. She sat down beside him and rested a hand on his shoulder.

"I tried to find you," he said. "I thought you might be able to get me an ass or a litter . . . anything . . . so I could go with David. But the guards were all through the corridors. I couldn't get to David. And then they tramped on my foot. I had to crawl."

Michal pressed his shoulder and ran her hand through his hair. "You wanted to go with David?"

"Yes . . . yes . . ."

"He may no longer be King, and little protection for you."

"I don't care. I want to be with him!"

"You love him, don't you?"

"Yes."

Michal shook her head, and murmured, "So strange, that man. What he can do to people."

Mephibosheth reared up on an elbow. "He loved my father."

"For a time. Yes. That was so."

"Even now. He talks about it. He sings about it."

"Distant times . . . they grow golden."

"And Jonathan loved him."

"For a time. Yes. That was so."

Mephibosheth lay back on the pallet, his eyes on the ceiling. "Tell me stories of Jonathan, my father."

Michal looked at the shaft of light coming in the window, thought of the distant times grown golden, and started to talk.

Jonathan. He had been nine years older than Michal, and her first memory of him was how he shattered the quiet of the tent with his boisterous laughter. She had looked up—she couldn't have been more than five—and there was Jonathan, gawky in his youth, but tall and powerful. His leather sling-shot was tucked into the belt of his tunic, and slung over his shoulders he proudly held a dead gazelle, which he presented to his mother, Ahinoam, with an awkward bow. "One shot, Mother. I hit it with one shot!" Ahinoam had taken the gift graciously.

Thinking back on the incident now, Michal could feel a wistful amusement. The King's table groaned with lamb and beef and cheese and fruits. But Ahinoam had skinned the young gazelle herself, roasted it, and served it for Jonathan's pride. He was her eldest son.

As she had grown, Michal always saw Jonathan with a bow slung over his shoulder and a quiver of arrows. She'd follow him outside where he had a piece of wood set against a stone down in a gulch, and she'd watch him shoot arrow after arrow into the wood until the feathers of the arrows seemed to bristle in a birdlike thicket. Exultant, he'd pick her up, toss her into the air, and catch her as she shrieked with fright and laughter.

There was a big plane tree on the outskirts of the encampment at Gibeah. Jonathan would hoist her onto his back. She'd cling to him, arms around his neck and legs locked around his waist, as he climbed the tree, up through the branches till they found a sitting place where they could see the whole encampment through the leaves. The rhythms of the tents, pitched row on row. Soldiers lounging in front of the tents or marching down the roads between them. Caravans of camels and asses loaded with sacks and jars. Women in their dark and flowing robes gliding through the bustle and confusion. And over it all, like a cloud, dust . . . dust . . . dust.

Once Michal had asked Jonathan, high up in the tree, "Father's the best warrior in the world, isn't he?"

Jonathan shrugged. "Almost, I guess."

"How is that? God?"

"Maybe. But most of all, he beats everybody, and takes all their livestock and gold and things."

"Are you going to do that when you grow up?"

"I want to grow up to be a mighty warrior like father. That is what I want to do."

Michal remembered how he held his head and how his shoulders straightened when he said those words, and she remembered, now ruefully, the pride she had felt in the ambition that would lead to his death.

She remembered when he first went to battle, shoulder to shoulder with Saul, against the Philistines. He could not have been more than eighteen. He had come back with a rakish bandage around his head that he wore like a crown. He sat her on his knee and told her stories of the battle so wild that Michal had come to believe that all Philistines were at least seven feet high and breathed fire. But Saul and Jonathan had conquered them with the strength of the Lord.

She had loved Jonathan. Everybody had loved Jonathan. At evening meal, as the wine flowed, Jonathan would tell some story of battle, march, or encampment with an impish grin on his face. Saul would wrap a big paw around his son's shoulder, and the two of them would laugh in great bellows. As the laughter subsided, she could see the pride in Saul's eyes. She could also see how Ishbosheth fumed with jealousy. Still, he too seemed to know the wonder of Jonathan and tried to imitate his stride, his smile, his princely stance.

She could comb her memories for the happiness of those times. Then David came to Saul's court, the shepherd boy from Bethlehem.

THREE

As David neared the crest of Olivet, the pain in his back began to ease, and a cool breeze from the west stirred him from his torpor. He still had Joab. He had Bathsheba and Solomon. He had the mercenary guard. Across the Jordan in Gilead were friendly troops, loyal to him. The energies of his youth and maturity, the skills of his state-craft, the wiles of his political intelligence, his military acumen, all began to reassert themselves. David began to think.

The person he thought about most was his former counselor, now defected to Absalom—Ahithophel. Here was immediate danger that needed to be countered with speed. Ahithophel, at David's side, had been lethal to David's enemies. At Absalom's side, he could be lethal to David, and David knew it.

A strange man, Ahithophel. He reminded David of a serpent basking on a hot stone in the wilderness of Judea, seemingly drained of all life by the heat. Yet, in a sudden writhing serpentine action, he could strike with unfailing accuracy. David knew his counselors. If he wanted good reason for moderation and caution, he would turn to Hushai. If he wanted to know the advantages of precipitous action, he'd consult with Joab. But if he wanted to know what to do, when and where for maximum effect, he'd summon Ahithophel, who would sit there, nodding in the audience chamber, his eyes ominously drowsy while David explained the situation. Then his hands would begin to move, as if he touched the substance of the circumstances and molded them in thin air until they had a whole new shape and form. Then, with a quick flick of words, he'd strike at the vulnerable point in that new mold of circumstance, and leave David to ponder the precision of his devious mind. Ahithophel was a useful and dangerous man, and he wondered if Absalom had the sense to know it. Perhaps he could stir doubts in Absalom's mind. . . .

Sitting on a rock on the path up Olivet, David called for Hushai, who came with his tunic torn and dirt on his head. David, his anguish momentarily receding and intent on plans, brushed the earth out of Hushai's hair and looked him in the eye. "My friend, I want you to return to Jerusalem."

Hushai was aghast. "Jerusalem? And leave you here? Why?"

"You can serve me better in Jerusalem."

Hushai frowned. "How?"

"Ahithophel is in Jerusalem with Absalom. And Ahithophel, as we both know, is a counselor of great wisdom and guile. He can give Absalom advice which, if acted upon, might destroy us before we could reach the Jordan. We must frustrate his counsel."

Hushai nodded slowly. "Absalom is . . . impressionable."

"He would be impressed with you. Go to Jerusalem and say to him, 'I will be your servant; up to now I have been your father's servant, and now I will be yours.'"

"The words will gall me."

"If you love me, say them anyway." David paused and his voice lowered. "You will have with you the priests Zadok and Abiathar; tell them everything that you hear in Absalom's household. Through them you can pass on to me everything you hear."

Hushai stood, bowed to the King—his King—and squared his shoulders. But his eyes glowed with warmth. "I shall miss you, my Lord."

David offered a hand to Hushai, who took it in a firm grip. "It may not be long until we see each other again."

"I shall pray so."

As Hushai turned to go, David called him back. "One thing. Find out how it goes with Mephibosheth."

"I will, my Lord."

Hushai started down the path toward Kidron. David followed him with his eyes until he disappeared among the upward marching troops. Then, wearily, he got to his feet to climb to the crest of Olivet.

Lord, how my enemies have multiplied! Many rise up against me; there are many who say, "God will not bring him victory." As he looked at the crest of Olivet above him, he thought, *I cry aloud to the Lord, and He answers me from His holy mountain. But would He? And what would His answer be? That the Lord had found pleasure in Absalom, and David was cast from the Lord's sight?*

He remembered hearing how the prophet Samuel had cursed Saul for not obeying the commands Samuel had received from the Lord, and how Saul had returned to Gibeah in gloom. David had known those glooms of Saul. He felt the gloom now within himself. It was as if the sky had gone dark, and time moldered. Now he ached for Saul, for the loneliness that corroded the spirit, the loneliness that David, as a youth, had tried to assuage.

Three of David's older brothers—Eliah, Abinadab, and Shammah—were in Saul's service as warriors when David was in Bethlehem, tending the sheep of his father, Jesse, as they grazed in the dry hills of Judea. In his solitude

24

under the hot sky, David played his harp to keep himself company, drawing music from the sound of the wind, the beat of rain, the bleating of sheep, the pulse of his heart. He'd sit there, letting his music drift into the yielding air, miles from Bethlehem, and wonder at the world his brothers shared at Saul's court in Gibeah—the great feasts, the marches and battles, the shining glory of the King himself.

When his brothers returned to visit their father, he would question them eagerly about what it was like in Gibeah with the King. They looked so strange and powerful with their armor, helmets, and swords, and he imagined them striking terror into the hearts of the Philistines.

After evening meal, he would play his harp for them, while Jesse sat there and smiled with pride. David played with special gusto and was warmed by the shining of his brothers' eyes. They brought news of the King's court; he brought news of the wide sky; and they shared the wonderments among them.

Then one day, while his brothers were visiting and the whole family was together, a strange thing happened. David was fifteen at the time.

There was a flurry in Bethlehem. A messenger arrived to say that the prophet Samuel would be arriving that afternoon from Ramah in the north to make a sacrifice to the Lord. The messenger urged the elders of the town, and particularly the household of Jesse, to join in the sacrifice.

All of which was puzzling to the elders. They knew of Samuel's curse on Saul, and they knew that Saul, once Samuel left the protection of Ramah, might seek him out and kill him. Yet here was Samuel, coming to Bethlehem. They decided that Samuel must be on very holy business indeed.

Samuel came with a heifer, a horn of oil, a ritual knife, and a retinue of Levites. He proceeded to the stone altar, followed by the elders, who made nervous inquiries. "Why have you come? Is all well?"

The old prophet waved them aside. "All is well. I have come to sacrifice to the Lord. Hallow yourselves and come with me to the sacrifice."

At the stone altar, Samuel had the bound heifer laid before him on the raised surface, its legs kicking, its eyes big with fear. Samuel raised his eyes to the sky, then took the ritual knife and plunged it into the heifer's throat. Blood spurted over the stone and over Samuel's robes. Grunting with effort, Samuel split the carcass open and reached into the still-pulsing cavity. His hands, bright with the blood of this shared offering, carefully extracted the fat from around the animal's entrails, the two kidneys from behind its haunches and the larger lobe of its liver, and heaped them upon the carcass, ready for the fire. As the smoke curled up to the heavens, carrying with it the pungent odor of the ritual of God, Samuel prayed.

A Levite brought a bowl of water to the prophet, and he washed the blood off his hands, muttering holy words as he did so. Fingering his horn of oil, he turned and faced the Bethlehemites assembled near the altar. "I seek a son of the household of Jesse."

Jesse came forward and bowed low. "I have eight sons, prophet."

"Bring them to me, one by one."

As each son came forward, Samuel looked at him with unblinking, penetrating eyes and then shook his head. Jesse grew steadily more disappointed that none of his sons seemed to find favor with the prophet. When the seventh son had passed before him, Samuel turned to Jesse. "You said you had eight sons. Where is the eighth?"

Jesse was embarrassed. "He is only a youth, prophet. He is at home, tending the sheep."

Samuel's voice was urgent. "Bring him to me."

David had known nothing of this until Shammah came to him at the sheep-fold. Shammah looked at David as if he had never seen him before. "The prophet Samuel wants to see you."

David blinked. "Me?"

"Yes. You."

"Why?" He wiped his dirty hands on his tunic.

"When the prophet Samuel asks to see you, you don't ask why. You go." And Shammah brushed the tunic where David had wiped his hands and ran his hand through David's hair to smooth it. "Now, come."

David pulled back. "But . . . this lamb . . . I was just . . ."

"Never mind the lamb! Let's go." Taking David by the hand, he led him into the presence of Samuel before the altar, the carcass of the heifer still smoking on the stone behind him. The odor was acrid in David's nostrils.

He looked at Samuel, and felt a tingling awe. In Samuel's eyes, he thought he saw all the resonances of the wide sky, thunder and the flash of storm, the searing force of sunlight, and the mysteries of nightfall. Below the eyes were lips, barely visible in the tightness and aging of the face. His vision followed the sparse gray beard down to the robe, its whiteness drenched with blood.

David imagined the body beneath, sinewed like a lion. He felt himself powerless. Yet, sprung upon and possessed, David felt he could gather to himself the power of the infinite. He could call down upon himself the sky to which he sang, and grasp lightning in his hand.

Samuel stepped toward him, his hand on the horn of oil. "This is the one," he said, his eyes holding David motionless. Samuel put his thumb in the horn of oil, and then reached out and pressed it against David's forehead. His voice was tense and low. "Let the spirit of the Lord be upon you."

David felt as if the whole sky poured into him through Samuel's touch, and he shivered.

As Samuel drew back, David looked around at his father and brothers. They were watching him intently. Not one came forward to him. They stood there, as they might have stood before the Ark.

27

David suddenly felt alone and afraid. He had heard the story of Joseph and his brothers, how they had thrown Joseph down a well and sold him into slavery in Egypt. Now David's brothers stood around him, and he wondered what they thought of his blessing from Samuel. It had not come to any of them. Only to him. Just as Joseph had been specially favored. Would he also be specially hated?

The dread grew so strong that he nearly turned to Samuel to plead that he take back the blessing. *I am unworthy and not fit for special favor.* But something stopped him. How did he know who he was? If Samuel acted on God's commands, was the force of his touch not just a blessing but a sign of Divine Will? And who was David, for all his dread, to deny that Will?

He reached up and touched the oily spot on his forehead. What was it there for? Why had this Will singled him out?

A quick change of the wind sent the smoke of the burning carcass swirling about him, so opaque that he could barely see. The smoke made him cough, and filled his eyes with tears, clouding his vision further. The figure of Samuel was blurred and ghostlike, some demon apparition from the fires of the earth that had left its mark upon him. He fought panic, and groped his way to his father. Then he sensed his brothers gathering around him. Shammah laid a hand on one shoulder. Eliah patted his back. He looked from one to the other, tears streaming down his face. "Why . . . why did Samuel do that?" he asked.

But no one answered.

One evening, later that year, David was practicing with his sling against a tree trunk outside Jesse's house. He felt he needed the practice because he had nearly hit the eye of a wandering sheep the day before. A good shepherd planted the pebble just about a hand's breadth in front of the sheep's nose to turn it back to the flock. But at twenty paces, David had missed, and he felt ashamed of himself.

He faced the tree trunk at twenty-five paces, and shot pebbles at its rounded surface. If the pebble deflected to right or left, he had missed his mark. But if the pebble bounced straight back at him, he was on target.

He had shot more than a score of pebbles with only three deflections when he noticed two men coming up the road on asses. As they drew nearer to the house, David recognized his older brother Shammah, followed by a stranger wearing a feathered helmet. Dropping his sling, he ran to meet them, apprehensive about the reason for this visit.

"What brings you here?" David asked.

Shammah, his armor flashing in the rays of the setting sun, straightened his shoulders. "We come on a mission to Jesse from Saul the King." He reached out and rumpled David's hair. "You better come along with us."

David felt the same tingling of awe he had felt when he had first seen Samuel. His own brother Shammah had come on a mission from the mighty King of Israel and Judah, and had come with a warrior at his side. Still, he wondered. "No harm has come to Eliah or Abinadab?"

"Oh, no. They are well. They send their greetings. It is just that I was selected for this mission to our father. I bring Benaiah, here, of the Royal Guard . . ." pointing to the man with the plumed helmet, ". . . to deliver the King's message."

David could not imagine what the message was, or whom in his sleepy little shepherds' village it could concern. And what did this strange soldier have to do with it? He looked Benaiah directly in the eye, and the gaze was returned just as directly. David felt a strange understanding with this man. He realized that Benaiah was not much older than he was, yet he could only respect the assurance reflected in his person, his gear, his trappings. But he was startled to see, in Benaiah's eyes, the respect returned. What did Benaiah see in him, a youth in a dirty shepherd's tunic? Yet in Benaiah's eyes, the deference was there.

29

David walked beside Shammah till they came to the courtyard of Jesse's house, and the two men dismounted. As Benaiah was tethering his ass, Shammah drew David aside and spoke in a low urgent voice. "Do not tell Benaiah or anyone else of your anointment by Samuel. It would offend Saul."

"But . . . but . . . I do not know the King."

"You will," said Shammah. "You will." And he put a protective arm around David's shoulder.

David, more confused than ever, entered the house of Jesse behind Shammah and Benaiah.

Jesse embraced Shammah and kissed him. Then he turned and looked at Benaiah with awe. But Benaiah was unfazed. He stood statuesque, in military stance, the feathers of his helmet nearly touching the beams of the ceiling, and David felt the presence of mysterious royalty fill the room.

Jesse beckoned to one handmaiden to bring water so the travelers could wash their feet. He sent a slave for wine and bread to feed the visitors. He bid the two men be seated and take their ease. Shammah did so, but Benaiah remained standing, as if he were held by some invisible discipline.

Shammah turned to Jesse. "Father, Benaiah brings a message from Saul, the King, at Gibeah."

Jesse blanched. His voice was barely above a whisper. "Does it go well with Eliah and Abinadab?"

Shammah patted his father's knee. "They are well in the King's service. It is another matter."

Jesse's hands twitched. "We have paid our just tribute."

"Benaiah brings a blessing to our house."

"Oh?" Jesse looked at Benaiah's erect, impeccable figure with caution. "Tell us the blessing Saul sends us."

Benaiah bowed slightly, glanced at David, and drew from his belt two sticks wound in a crisp clothlike material. He pulled the sticks apart, spreading the sheet between. David glanced at the sheet surreptitiously. There were black

30

markings on it. David had never seen such a thing before.

Benaiah cleared his throat and in a sing-song voice with traces of an alien accent began to recite, his eyes following the markings on the sheet.

"It has been brought to the attention of Saul, King of Israel and Judah, by his worthy warriors, Eliah, Abinadab, and Shammah, that their brother David is much skilled in the playing of the harp and the singing of poetry. It is the King's pleasure that he should have as part of his court a royal musician who, by the gentleness of his music, may assuage the King's many tribulations. It is therefore requested of Jesse of Bethlehem that his son, David, shall come to the King's court at Gibeah, and serve Israel and Judah with his skill of music as his brothers Eliah, Abinadab, and Shammah so bravely serve by their skill of arms."

David glanced at Shammah. There was a faint grin on Shammah's face, and he gave David a barely perceptible wink.

Benaiah continued. "My Lord, the King, wishes an answer to his request, for I must return immediately to Gibeah."

Jesse, frowning, adjusted the sleeves of his robe. "It is near nightfall. You are welcome here for lodging till the morning."

"The moon is high. The way is straight and swiftly traveled," said Benaiah. "And the King is a man of brisk decision."

Silence pulsed in the room.

Jesse turned to David. "Would you like to go?"

"To the King's court?" David's eyes glistened. "Yes."

Jesse's eyes clouded with sadness. He spoke to Benaiah. "He is only a boy. He has not been away from Bethlehem."

Shammah broke in. "We will care for him. Eliah, Abinadab, and I. He would be our pride in the court."

But Jesse kept looking at Benaiah. "Would it be the King's pleasure that he could return to Bethlehem from time to time to visit us?"

31

Benaiah's voice no longer had a military clip. "The King's power is tempered with understanding. I serve him, and I know."

Another silence.

David flung himself into Jesse's lap. "Father, I want to go."

He felt Jesse's grasp on his shoulder, a grasp of strength he had felt since childhood. He did not want to pull away. But he said again: "Father, I want to go."

He saw tears in Jesse's eyes as his father said, "It is an honor for my son. He may go."

Benaiah bowed. "I shall tell the King that Shammah will bring him before two sundowns." And he left.

David lay on the pallet beside Shammah in the darkness and asked, "What kind of man is Saul?"

Shammah was silent for a moment. Then he said, his voice solemn, "He is the greatest man of the tribes of Jacob."

"Greater than Abraham? Greater than Moses?"

"He has brought us to become a people. A people among peoples. And we can hold our heads high before them. Because Saul holds his head highest. The law we have learned. The tradition we live by. But at the time of the Judges we lived in our weakness as we would. Through Saul we came to know the power of the Lord."

"But Samuel . . . ?"

Shammah flared. "A crazy old man, jealous that he spoke for the Lord. But Saul has acted for the Lord. And through him, Israel and Judah have a king." Shammah's voice turned to a growl. "Let Samuel molder with his curses in Ramah. We serve the Lord."

David stirred on his pallet, staring into the darkness. "Shammah?"

"Yes?"

"When Samuel anointed me, what did that mean?"

"Your brothers and I talked of that. Samuel was a great

judge. A great prophet. But the clouds of his old age close in upon him. Perhaps, when he saw you, there was a break in the clouds, and his vision was clear. But what vision? For what purpose? We do not know. But if the spirit of the Lord is within you, then we, as your kin, can share whatever greatness can come to you. That is what we thought. That is why we urged upon Saul that you come to his court."

David turned close to Shammah, buried his head in Shammah's neck and stretched his arm across Shammah's chest. "Shammah. You frighten me."

Shammah tousled David's hair. "Do not fret yourself, child. Perhaps Samuel is as mad as we think he is."

But David was restless. Lying there in the darkness, he had visions of Saul the King, taller than Benaiah, strong as an Egyptian bull, sheathed in golden armor, with eyes as blazing as Samuel's. What could his music say to such a man? What solace could he offer such crushing strength?

"Shammah?"

"Yes?"

"Benaiah said that the King has 'many tribulations.' What does that mean?"

"Worries. Problems. Things that bother him. Decisions that have to be made, and sometimes the decisions . . . well . . . they are hard to make."

"But the King has all that power. He can make people do what he wants them to do. Is not that so?"

Shammah sighed. "No. It is not always so. Even with guards and armies, it is not always so. And when he cannot have his will, a darkness comes over him. He strikes out. Sometimes at the wrong people. Sometimes at the wrong time. It is hard to be a king. I have seen him suffer. I have come to him when he is alone in his tent, his shoulders stooped, his eyes like a dog's. I leave quickly. I don't want to see him like that. Because he is the great Saul, and the King of our people. But you will see him like that, and through your music, perhaps you can bring him back to himself. "

33

David felt fear again. He thought of his flocks, his dog, his sling, and the silence of the barren hills. The marauding wild dogs and lions that stalked the straying sheep. He knew the silence of the night and the gleam of firelight that pushed the darkness away, but it still surrounded him, with unknown danger lurking. He had known fear, as natural as the wind and moonlight. But the fear of Saul had a sting to it. The unknown he now faced flashed with consuming fires that might destroy him. He would be at the mercy of mysteries like Samuel's eyes, and the acrid smoke of burning carcasses. What could his harp do against a grasping flame?

Yet flame was power—light to signal and attract. He knew the flames the shepherds lit on the tops of Judean hills so the flocks could gather and find safety at nightfall. Shepherds and their dogs could take turns standing watch in the darkness, warmed by the kindled fire, listening for sounds of danger, ready to rouse the whole encampment to protect the flocks.

Saul was the flame of Israel and Judah. He lit the sky and gathered the tribes against the dangers of the night. But listening to Shammah talk, David wondered if the strength of Saul's flame consumed Saul himself. Was he a burning carcass? David ached at the thought of the charred flesh, the disfigurements hidden beneath a sheath of gold.

Jesse lay on his pallet that night, and thought of his son, David. If David went to Gibeah, he would have to hire another sheepherder for his flock. Perhaps one of his sister's children . . . But David was a good shepherd who rarely lost an animal. With David in the hills, Jesse felt confident that his flock was safe and cared for, and he was not sure he would feel that way with any of his sister's children, even though some of them were older than David. His brother-in-law liked his wine; his sister liked to talk; and the children ran wild. Still, they were his family. Better than hiring some undependable Canaanite.

But the sadness Jesse felt was not just for his flock. David, his youngest, would be leaving home—the last of his sons and his favorite. He knew the child was comely and pleasing to the Lord. But he had never felt, until Samuel had anointed the boy, the specialness of the son he was about to lose. David was made for greater things than shepherding in Bethlehem, and he would bow to the Lord's Will. But he was old and he was sad.

The house of Jesse bustled the next morning with preparations for Shammah and David's leaving for the court at Gibeah. The doubt had left Jesse's eyes, and he looked on David with an almost reverent pride. His other sons were warriors among warriors, but David, he felt, was destined for the King's inner circle, a companion and solace to the King himself. So more honor would come to the house of Jesse. So more favor would come to Bethlehem, and protection against the Amalekites and the Philistines.

Jesse ordered the maidservants to wash David's best tunics and cloaks, and to pack them. He called in his head manservant and conferred with him on the stock and stores from which he could make an offering to the King. The figs were good that year, but the wine was better, and the best of the goats had recently produced a kid. After solemn consideration, Jesse decided that David and Shammah should take a skin of wine, a homer of bread, and the kid as offerings to the King. The mules loaded, Shammah and David set off on the road north to Gibeah. As they made their way, David felt a tingling fear, and the easy confidence of Shammah could not still it. He could almost see Samuel walking ahead of them, leading David into an awesome unknown.

❀   ❀   ❀

35

David and Shammah sat close together on a bench outside Saul's massive tent. David clutched his harp, occasionally running his fingers across the strings and tightening the draw pegs to make sure the tuning was right. Beside them the asses loaded with the wine and bread brayed and shifted their hooves on the dusty earth. The sun was hot and David felt trickles of sweat on his cheeks and shoulders. He wondered if they'd show on his clean tunic. It was his best, with red piping carefully sewn around the neck and at the lower edge well above his knees. Shammah had seen to it that his sandals and thongs were carefully polished with sheep fat, and they shone in the sunlight. His hair was combed and he had seen its dark, curly luster in the silver mirror after Shammah had dressed it.

But for all the care that Shammah had given him, David still felt like an awkward shepherd boy lost in a world that might engulf him. He drew only one small solace during the tension of waiting for an audience with the King. Soldiers moved in and out of the royal tent. Some of them glanced at him as he sat on the bench; and some of those glances were as intimate as a caress, combing his body from head to foot with attentive eyes. Confronted with those glances, he at first turned his eyes to the ground and only sensed the heat of their attention. But later, with one or two of the passing soldiers, he met their gazes with his own and even shifted his body slightly so that the tunic rose a bit. He hoped that Shammah did not notice.

But he found himself enjoying the game. People were paying attention to him, even in the great capital of Gibeah. He had the power to draw eyes to himself. Back in Bethlehem, a workaday, work-stained shepherd boy, he had never felt such power. But what did they know of him here? Only a groomed, strange youth who might be harpist to the King. He felt now an aura of royalty that might perfume his person. On the bench, outside the tent of Saul, he was so close . . .

Benaiah came out of the royal tent, radiant in the sunlight

36

and looking taller than ever. He walked toward them with a light-footed ease. As Benaiah approached Shammah and David, Shammah rose and bowed and David hastily followed his brother's lead.

Shammah gestured to the asses. "A skin of the best wine for the King."

"He will be grateful," Benaiah said. "He has been expecting you."

"And a homer of bread. And the best kid of our goat herd." He stroked the goat's ears. "All from Jesse of Bethlehem in gratitude for the honor to his son."

Benaiah nodded formally. "The King will be most pleased." But he turned his full attention to David. "The King is anxious to hear the music of your harp. He has had a tiring day." And he gestured toward the entrance to the tent. Shammah turned to follow, but Benaiah tactfully stood in his way. "I believe that the King would wish to hear the musician alone."

Shammah was flustered. "Yes. Of course. Better to judge him. Alone. I shall wait here."

David turned and grasped Shammah's hand for just a moment. Then Benaiah opened the flap of the tent, and David, alone, entered the presence of Saul.

After hours in brilliant sunlight, David felt blinded in the darkness of the tent. His eyes focused on a few flickers of lamplight. Then he discerned a massive figure across the tent, sitting on a chair, one hand held against its forehead. The figure was barely more than a shadow, but he sensed a huge power in that presence, and as if drawn by its magnetism, he took, almost unknowingly, a few hesitant steps toward it. Here was mystery as vibrant as Samuel, as big as a thunderous sky.

The voice of the figure was as hard and rough as weathered stone. "You are David of Bethlehem."

"Yes, my Lord."

"Come closer."

David stepped into the lamplight, just over an arm's reach

37

from Saul, and stood there, fighting quivers of fear, his eyes downcast. He felt Saul's gaze upon him, more probing than those of the soldiers who had passed him outside the tent.

Finally Saul spoke. "You are fairest of the house of Jesse. Fairest, perhaps, in all of Judah."

David still quivered, but fear was now mixed with excitement in the closeness to that virile strength. The words wrapped him in a languorous warmth—"fairest of the house of Jesse." Those had been the King's words, a voice out of the mystery of the darkness, just as Samuel had spoken out of the smoke of the burnt offering. For David, the mysteries congealed into one question. "What does God want of me? What is the price for His gifts?"

Saul's voice—so commanding it was no command: "Sit down and play your harp for me and sing your songs. The sweetness may lighten my head." And he pressed the fingers of his big hand against his temples.

David sat cross-legged on the rug in front of Saul's chair, and rested the base of his harp on one bare knee. He ran his fingers softly over the strings of the harp, not daring to look at Saul's big body high before him, tightened a few draw pegs, and then, in a burst of chords, began to sing.

Make a joyful noise unto the Lord, all ye lands.
    Serve the Lord with gladness:
    come before his presence with singing.
Know ye that the Lord he is God:
    it is he that hath made us, and not we ourselves;
    we are his people, and the sheep of his pasture.
Enter into his gates with thanksgiving,
    and into his courts with praise:
    be thankful unto him, and bless his name.
For the Lord is good;
    his mercy is everlasting;
    and his truth endureth to all generations.

The final chords were lost in the muffled silence of the

tent. Saul was silent and motionless, his fingers still holding his temples. David waited, barely breathing.

Finally Saul stirred. "You have a strange God, young man. Where did you find Him?"

"In the hills. Mostly at daybreak."

Saul grunted. " 'Everlasting mercy,' eh? It would be a sad day for us if that included the Philistines."

"I wasn't thinking of the Philistines."

Saul's voice lowered to a growl. "I was." But David thought he saw, in the faint lamplight, just the trace of a grin cross Saul's face.

Saul moved his big hand, as if to push aside disturbing thoughts. "No more of this 'everlasting mercy.' Your harp plays its own gladness. Play more for me. Just the music."

David was somewhat abashed. He was proud of his songs. But Saul wanted only music, and who was to argue with Saul? David played before the King, there in the lamplight, till Saul's hand dropped from his temples and made vague gestures to the rhythm of the music, his eyes looking distant.

David watched Saul, whose head was now held high, and he realized that, however dark his spirits, however heavy his burdens, Saul was a magnificent man who wore his kingship as David's imagined gold. To young David, Saul was radiant in both his power and his person.

Saul asked, "Where is your brother, Shammah?"

"I think he is still waiting outside the tent."

"Guard!"

Out of a dark corner of the tent came a man with a feathered helmet who looked like Benaiah, though he was not as tall. David hadn't even noticed that he was there in the shadows, until he emerged to stand before the King.

"Go and get Shammah of Bethlehem and bring him to me."

The guard bowed and left the tent. As he opened the flap, a shaft of harsh sunlight cut through the darkness and made Saul's armor glisten, but his face was still in shadow.

The flap opened agan, and Shammah bowed to the King. Saul beckoned him forward. Shammah advanced toward the King's seat with a soldierly pace that David had never noticed before, and stood erect at a respectful distance. So, David thought, this was how it was for a soldier in the King's service. He wasn't, David had to admit, as impressive as Benaiah, but he was, without doubt, a warrior waiting orders from his king.

But Saul neither growled nor barked. His voice was almost gentle. "I am pleased with your brother David. His music cuts the gloom. Present my compliments to your father, Jesse, and ask of him that David stay in my service —always with my permission to visit Bethlehem when he wills. But before you return to Bethlehem, Shammah, take David to the tent of Ishbosheth that he may share it with my son. They are about the same age. . . ." He paused, and sighed. "Young David here has grace . . . and wit . . . and even some evidence of thought. Perhaps he might do Ishbosheth some good."

Shammah stammered in confusion. "My Lord, Prince Ishbosheth is . . . I mean . . . gifted greatly by your fatherhood. Young David . . . a mere shepherd boy . . . could learn of the world from the prince."

Saul looked balefully at Shammah. "No need to babble on, Shammah. Even kings know their families. Just do my bidding." And David caught that trace of a smile cross Saul's lips again. Who was this Saul? What hid behind that mask of dourness? David had the sudden image of a great bear, poking and cuffing his cubs with exasperated affection.

Shammah brought him to Ishbosheth's tent. The flap was open, and daylight streamed into the tent's recesses. As Shammah and David entered, a lanky figure rose from the pallet with awkward motions and stared at them with curiosity.

Shammah bowed. "My Prince. We have come from the King's tent. I bring my brother David who, for the King's pleasure, will be the court's musician. It is the King's desire that David share your tent with you so that you can teach him the ways of the court."

Ishbosheth appeared bewildered. "I . . . teach your brother . . . the ways of the court?" He gave a mirthless laugh. "Saul jests. I see the court through a dog's eyes, waiting in corners, grateful for a tossed bone."

Shammah protested. "You are hard on yourself, Ishbosheth. You have the respect due a prince."

Ishbosheth shook his head. "You Bethlehemites always have oil on your tongues so the words just slither out. Jonathan is the prince, and you know it."

The whip-crack in Ishbosheth's voice reduced Shammah to a momentary fluster. "Still . . ." he murmured.

Ishbosheth turned to David. "Still . . ." he echoed Shammah, "you are welcome to my kennel." He grinned, and it was a sad grin like Saul's. "We bark a lot around here. But we don't bite."

David decided he liked Ishbosheth. But who was Jonathan?

David lay on a pallet on one side of the tent, while Ishbosheth lay on the other. It was night. David could hear the guards talking in low voices outside. The sound of voices was strange to him. No guards patrolled Jesse's house in Bethlehem. But at Gibeah, guards in their feathered helmets were everywhere, impassive in their watches. And David was living in the tent of a prince.

It was hard to think of Ishbosheth as so exalted. His movements never seemed decisive but always a little off balance. He walked with a slouch. His voice had a dry, ironic crackle.

At eighteen, he was tall, almost as tall as Saul, but his body was gangly; his face was lean and pocked, with only a straggle of a beard. He had a large mole on his left cheek. David could understand—reluctantly—why Saul might not consider Ishbosheth a masterpiece. But Ishbosheth's view of himself and the world around him seemed to give him a strength that was deceptive in its suppleness. David had seen Ishbosheth silence Shammah with a flick of words. Now that they were alone together, Ishbosheth could tilt one eyebrow and in a sentence, even a phrase, hit a target as precisely as a slung pebble. Dog's eyes he might have at court, but they were pitilessly watchful.

"Jonathan?" Ishbosheth's voice sounded weary in the darkness. "Well, it is my thought that God created Jonathan just to shame the rest of mankind."

"What do you mean?"

Ishbosheth sighed. "My sister, Michal, and I, we talk about it. She looks in the silver of her mirror, and she sees what she sees. I look in the silver of my mirror, and I see what you see. People. Mere people. With the blemishes most people have. The ordinary creations of a casual God. But then we look at Jonathan, just as our father looks at Jonathan, and we wonder . . . how could this be? If God is capable of such perfect creation, why is He so careless with the rest of us?"

In the lamplight, David saw Ishbosheth rear himself on one elbow and stare across the tent at David. "When I saw you come here with Shammah, I had the same thought. How could this be? Another perfect creation." He settled back on the pallet again. "But you are young. God may be merciful to you and mark you with the blemishes of the rest of us."

David thought of Samuel. David thought of Saul. David thought of the terrible powers that caressed him. And suddenly he envied Ishbosheth his deformities. "I hope so," he said.

"Do not hope too heavily." Ishbosheth yawned. "God,

perhaps, is jealous of His perfections and saves them for His own mysterious purposes."

The evening meal took place inside Saul's great tent. All afternoon, maidservants turned the spits of lamb and kid carcasses over smoky coals in front of the tent, and as the afternoon sun began to fade, manservants brought in skins of wine, figs, dates, grapes, and loaves of bread in clay bowls to set upon the rugs that covered the tent floor.

Ishbosheth and David walked past the King's tent as all these preparations were in progress. With a quick movement, Ishbosheth pulled a chunk of meat from one of the roasting carcasses. The maidservant turning the spit let out a squawk of outrage, but Ishbosheth, the meat in hand, quickened his step and led David around the corner of the tent. Safely out of sight, Ishbosheth grinned. "You have to fight for what you get around here."

He pulled the meat apart and handed half to David. They hunched on the ground and chewed on the meat like a couple of Amalekite brigands. The food tasted all the better.

Nothing in David's experience in Bethlehem had prepared him for the evening ceremony of the great feast in the royal tent. Jesse's house at Bethlehem, like Saul's old house in Gibeah, was a house—or rather a collection of mud-brick rooms added haphazardly around a central hall as Jesse's family had grown. From a distance the house looked like an outcropping of earth in curious crystalline rectangles, surrounded by sheep-folds, goat pens, and paddocks for the asses. David had lived in a busy mix of humans and animals with care and growth as the crux of life. Even his harp seemed a little superfluous.

Jesse's family ate their evening meal at a long table made of slabs of cedar. Other slabs served as benches on either side of the table. There the family gathered, first for prayer, and then for food served in simple clay bowls and mugs.

43

The fare was as simple as the clay it was served in. Bread was the staple; wine the drink; dates, figs, olives, and perhaps a roast lamb—although one lamb didn't go very far in Jesse's numerous family. The talk was low-keyed and decorous. Jesse, as patriarch, enforced that code. And when the eating was done, it was back to chores for everyone as long as daylight lasted. Evening meal at Jesse's house was as plain as the earth, and as nurturing, but not very memorable.

But when David walked into Saul's tent with Ishbosheth, once the cymbals had called the court to evening meal, he felt as if he were entering some magic barbaric land in Egypt or beyond the Great Sea. The blazing lamplight picked up all the hues and complex figures of the rugs that were strewn around the floor of the tent—the reds and greens, the azures and sunburst yellows. Set on the rugs were gold and silver and copper vessels, burnished until they glistened in the lamplight. Their strange designs and inlaid jewels added to their luster. Great bowls of polished wood gave a muted gleam of opulence. David gazed about the tent, and had a dark thought. No such things could be found in Judea; nor had he heard of such things in Israel. Saul's tent, set for the evening meal, must be the reward of pillage. He wondered who had died trying to defend the gold goblet over there, or the silver salver near his feet. All this in a tent that could be struck the next day, and serve as Saul's headquarters in Gilead or Beersheba. What more grandeur to the tent's furnishings might be added by the spilling of Ammonite or Amalekite blood?

Ishbosheth led David to a certain spot on the tent floor. "Here is where we have our meal."

David looked around. No chair or bench. Ishbosheth sat down on the thickly woven rug and bade David sit down beside him.

That certain spot. David watched others—strangers, all of them—enter the tent and find, as assuredly as Ishbosheth, their own certain spots. He wondered how they could tell one from another, but they all seemed to know. David looked around, assessing the spot to which Ishbosheth had led him in relation to all the other spots . . . and to the throne.

The tent area was nearly square, with the tent-cloth supported by twelve poles set in three rows. In the center of one side of the square was the main entrance—two great opening flaps. Directly across from the entrance, on a carpeted dais perhaps a hand's breadth high, was Saul's chair. The back and arms were ornately figured with such curious artistry that David concluded that this, too, was booty. Did Saul rule Israel and Judah from a throne carved by an enemy? As it stood now, the chair, even empty, seemed to dominate the whole tent. Like Saul, it was larger than life, and all else seemed to focus in relationship to it. On either side of the chair on the dais were thick, leather-covered cushions. David wondered what it would feel like to sit on one of those cushions at the very side of the King. Perhaps . . . when the King wanted him to play his harp. . . . But David thought again. If he sat on the cushion, the chair's arm would be between them.

Sitting beside Ishbosheth on the rug, close by one of the center tent-poles, David realized that they were close, but not all that close, to the throne. There was room for at least four or five more people between them and the dais in the central circle around the massive displays of food that the maidservants kept bringing in. David wondered. Ishbosheth was a prince. Why was he set so distantly from his father's side? Perhaps he was sharing the wrong tent with the wrong prince. Who was Jonathan? Where did he sit?

Suddenly David felt shame at the thought. Ishbosheth, in his wry and awkward way, had shown him kindness that invited trust. In the great world of Saul's court, David had found a friend. Was he to slough off so gentle an offering to pursue a sun-god—or whatever Jonathan was? He moved himself closer to Ishbosheth, and felt a solace of familiarity as he watched the gathering assemblage. Not counting the maidservants and male slaves bringing in the food and arranging it on trays and in vessels, David estimated that there must be almost twoscore men, women, and even a few children inside the tent. The men gravitated toward the center circles to eat together. The women and children gathered in the outer parts of the tent-space. Which was strange to David. At Bethlehem, everyone ate together. But this was no ordinary evening meal. Among the men he saw no genial relaxation after a day's hard work, but the foreboding tension of an evening's hard work.

"Who are these people?" David whispered to Ishbosheth.

Ishbosheth frowned. "It is hard to say. Aside from family, it keeps changing. Head men from the tribes and houses, Levites, generals, a prophet or two—although he doesn't like prophets—envoys from foreign lands, and now . . ." he grinned sidewise at David, ". . . even a harpist. They all make much of him, and he likes that. It keeps the evil spirits away from him. But my father is no fool. In all the chatter, he learns a lot, too. Strange. As the people prattle on, they don't realize how much they are telling him, or how well he may use the knowledge. He covers himself. You see, Saul has this way of gathering his brows and lowering them over his eyes. That is his frown. It can mean all sorts of things—curiosity, solemnity, puzzlement, or just an invitation to go on explaining the situation. That is his Frown of State. Quite harmless. Even endearing sometimes. But . . . but . . ." Ishbosheth tapped David on the knee, "Saul has another frown. Rather similar, but not quite. This is his Frown of the Evil Spirit. It comes when he has a stomach-ache, or when he feels that nobody loves him, or when he thinks too long on the Philistines . . . or even when he looks . . . just looks . . . at me."

"Oh, come, Ishbosheth. You are his son."

"Precisely. He doesn't like to be reminded, at least sometimes."

"But you are here . . . at the royal meal."

"And he would never have it otherwise. But, as you can see, not too close. Because when the Evil Spirit comes to

46

him, and he sees me and starts throwing things, he wants to be sure that he misses, or that I have time to dodge."

David sighed in wonderment. He could not imagine Jesse throwing anything at anybody. "What else does Saul do when he makes the Frown of the Evil Spirit?"

"Practically anything. Exile. Disinheritance. An occasional decapitation. Or a raid on some Philistine encampment. Nothing assuages Saul's Evil Spirit like Philistine blood."

"But Ishbosheth, there are Philistines all around us. The guards. Their feathered helmets are everywhere."

Ishbosheth lowered his voice. "They are not Philistines, but Cretans and Pelethites. The truth of the matter is Saul *likes* these uncircumcised warriors. They can read and write. They come from great cities and foreign lands across the Great Sea. They are smooth in their persons, witty in their talk, and loyal to the money he gives them. They try to teach him how to fight on the Philistine plains—not very well, I grant you—and Saul will probably never learn. But they do try."

David shook his head. "I do not understand. They are uncircumcised. They are unclean. They are to be scourged by the Lord!"

Ishbosheth gave David a baleful look. "There are two things one must learn quickly in the court of Saul. The first is not to take the priests and Levites too seriously. They have their own interests to protect, just like any other tribe of Jacob, but their interests may not be those of all the tribes. And Saul is the King of the twelve tribes of Israel and Judah. And it follows, for your personal safety, that you never mention the name of Samuel in Saul's presence, or you will evoke an entire army of Evil Spirits!"

"What is the other thing I must learn?"

"More difficult. Much more difficult. You must be able to distinguish between Saul's Frown of State and his Frown of the Evil Spirit."

David thought about that as he watched the hushed assembly, eyes glancing at the empty throne and then at the tent-flaps of the entrance. The food lay untouched in the gleaming vessels. Guards stood at the tent-flap entrance, as silent and impassive as idols.

David's voice was barely above a murmur. "But he also smiles."

"You've noticed that, eh?" Ishbosheth gave him a sharp glance. "Clever of you. He tries to hide it in his beard."

"Still . . ."

"Yes, he smiles. He used to smile a lot more, before he became King last year. Now he thinks it is undignified." Ishbosheth's shoulders sagged. "Too bad. Kingship, I think, is a disease. Power boils the brain. As long as Jonathan lives, I shall never be afflicted, and I am grateful for that. I am grateful, too, that I knew my father before he became King."

David looked at Ishbosheth as if he saw him for the first time. "You love your father, don't you?"

"Of course. As he loves me. I know that."

"But . . . you say . . ."

"David, my father is a warm man—even a passionate man. When he throws things at you, it is frequently a form of affection. If he exiles you, he only yearns to have you close to him. His curses are his blessings. His storms bring a gentle rain. If I did not know these things, I would be lost in Gilead or have found asylum with King Achish in Gath. But, as you see, I stay. I endure with him the afflictions of his kingship, even as I will attend Jonathan if the anguish passes to him."

David said, "I am blessed. Kingship will never come to me." But even as he said it, he felt the sting of the stare of Samuel's eyes and the smoke of the burning carcass.

There was a stirring at the tent-flaps. The guards went rigid. The eyes of people inside the darkness of the tent turned to the shaft of sunlight. In a sweep, Saul entered, clad in a robe of vermilion with a massive gold chain around his neck. As he started across the tent to the throne, he towered over all around him. He walked with a heavy, deliberate tread, and his eyes scanned the room as if he noted each face, each person.

Behind him walked two other men, each dressed in warriors' leather tunics, studded with silver and gold, and with leather thongs around their forearms. But they wore no swords. Only the Royal Guards wore swords. One of the men, was stocky, about Saul's age, with close-cropped, graying hair and scarred cheeks. He walked with an easy strut, and his chest broke the air before him like a ship's prow. The other of Saul's companions was much younger, and almost as tall as Saul himself. His hair was long and lustrous, his face and body a perfect symmetry. And he walked with a light-footed assurance that was just short of arrogant. David noticed the man's hands. He was fascinated by the mold of them and their sinewed strength. He kept looking at them as they swung beside the man's body. He wanted to touch them, and feel them touch him.

Saul came closer until his eyes stopped scanning and focused on David and Ishbosheth. David saw the smile, half-covered by Saul's beard, as he pointed a heavy finger at David's chest. "Take good care of my son Ishbosheth, and teach him well. He'll make a good sheepherder someday."

David gasped. Ishbosheth tightened his lips and blushed nearly purple. Saul passed by to take his seat on his throne. The older man took his seat on the leather cushion at the throne's left. The younger man sat on the cushion at the right. Everyone else, including David and Ishbosheth, sat down.

But as the food was passed to them by handmaidens, neither David nor Ishbosheth seemed to have any appetite. They sat there, shoulder to shoulder, and stared sightlessly ahead of them. Finally David whispered, "If Saul throws something at me, what will happen if I throw something back?"

Ishbosheth pondered that idea for a moment. "Well," he said judicially, "you might get your head cut off. Or he might just burst out laughing. Or, who knows? He might make you a general."

It was David's turn to ponder. But his mind kept veering off, thinking about those hands. "Ishbosheth . . . ?"

"Yes?"

"Who are the men on either side of Saul?"

"The older man on the left is Abner, Saul's commander-in-chief. The younger man on the right is . . ."

"I know," David murmured. "Jonathan."

But his eyes turned back to Saul.

Still leaning on Ira and Joab, David reached the crest of Olivet. The breeze from the west was cool on his forehead. All around him, the hills rose and descended, tawny in the sunlight. Above him was the arc of the sky, as vast as he had thought it as a youth, tending sheep in Judea. Then it had exalted him. Now it weighed upon him with its mystery. In its brightness, he felt revealed, every aching scar, and he yearned for mercy.

He looked across Kidron to Jerusalem. There he would have celebrated the Lord with a temple that would tower above Moriah. A place for the people. A place for the Ark. A place for the presence of the Lord. The battles he had won, the land he had conquered, the tribute from the trade routes that filled the royal coffers—all his acts as King would, he thought, serve that mighty purpose. But now the vision was only a desert mirage.

He looked down at the parched, dusty earth, as drained of life as he felt himself. He would mingle his dust with the dust beneath him.

He turned to Ira. "I must pray on the crest of Olivet. Prostrate myself to the Lord."

"It is the custom," Ira said, "but . . ." And he gripped David's quavering arm.

Joab exploded. "If you get down, with your back and all, what makes you think you'll ever be able to get up?"

David tightened his jaw. "I shall pray on Olivet."

He sank to his knees. Lion claws of pain raked his back until he cried out and flung himself full-length on the ground. His breathing came in gasps. Sweat poured off his face. The claws clenched his muscles to the bone and held as the pain shot, pulsed, throbbed through his body, wracking it with spasms. Each spasm filled his throat, like vomit, with another guttural cry that burst from his mouth.

He tried to move, to twist the pain away, but the claws grabbed again, thrusting him to the ground with new strength that made every breath a labor. His mouth was coated with the dust of the earth, and he could not move his head.

He heard Ira's voice, close to his ear. "My Lord. . . ." And felt a hand rest on his shoulder.

"Don't touch me!"

The hand hastily withdrew.

David's world had now shrunk to a womb of pain—all else shut out. His only reality was the ripping of his body by the bolts of shuddering force. A storm of all the sky had pressed into the small compass of his flesh, and he felt its rage within him.

He felt the claws give way a little. He lay perfectly still, barely breathing, not moving a muscle, like a hare beneath a bush nearby a lion stalking, and waited. The tension eased a little more, and his breathing grew more regular. But his face was still pressed to the dust, and he knew he must not move. He was a prisoner under the sky. He was shackled by the weakness of his flesh . . . his deeds . . . his history . . . his mortality. He could only wait. Wait? No. What? A burnt offering to fend off the rage that plundered his flesh? An incantation of word-magic to distract the lion from the hare beneath the bush? A sobbing of piety and a beating of breasts to placate the anger that swirled in the sky?

David had found another Being in the hills of Judea, the Being to which he played his harp and sang his poems.

Saul had swept his youthful visions aside with a wave of his big paw. Even Jonathan had been puzzled. "David, you *bargain* with God. You don't *talk* to Him. Who'd want to talk to anyone like that, anyway? All that thunder and thumping and rumbling commands. All that blood and destruction. You'd sing a song to *that*?"

But David's youthful vision stayed clear within him, and his songs varied as the winds and the weather and the wonderments of his soul.

Now, in the pit of his life, with no breath he could use even to utter the words, David sang a song that he and Mephibosheth had composed. He remembered the time. Mephibosheth had fallen. His crippled foot was swollen and aching. David was recovering from an arrow wound in his shoulder that still ached. They sat there, in the royal chamber, side by side, David with his harp, and lamented their miseries, their frailties, and the harshness of their God. So, in the dust, David now sang a soundless song:

O Lord, rebuke me not in thy wrath:
    neither chasten me in thy hot displeasure.
For thine arrows stick fast in me,
    and thy hand presseth me sore.
There is not soundness in my flesh because of thine anger;
    neither is there any rest
    in my bones because of my sin.
For mine iniquities are gone over mine head:
    as an heavy burden they are too heavy for me.
My wounds stink and are corrupt
    because of my foolishness.
I am troubled; I am bowed down greatly;
    I go mourning all day long.

David saw sandals of Cretan design close by. Moving his head slightly, he looked up and recognized Benaiah, now commander of the King's mercenaries. He gave Benaiah a frown of state and tried to hide a feeble smile beneath his beard. "I was happy enough as a shepherd, Benaiah. And I might have made a good poet. But *you* had to come along!"

"It was a blessing for Israel and Judah that I did," said Benaiah. "And now it is for me and Joab to get you to your feet."

David thought of the lion claws. "It is impossible. I will lie here till Absalom comes and cuts off my head. The way of it is quick and painless. And I am tired of pain. Leave me. Take the troops and cross the Jordan to Gilead. Let Absalom drink his fill of power. I have had my fill. I go to Sheol."

Benaiah did not answer. David sensed an ominous silence around him. He waited for the sound of a sword being drawn from its sheath. Perhaps Benaiah or Joab would save Absalom from patricide. But he heard no such sound.

The movements came so fast that David barely knew what was happening. Hands clenched both of his armpits and pulled upward with irresistible force. The lion claws wrenched at his back. He screamed in blinding pain. And then he realized that he was, miraculously, standing. Benaiah and Joab had him clamped between them. There was no way he could fall again.

Joab's voice was hard with command. "We have work to do, my Lord. Sheol will have to wait."

Step by step, leaning on Joab and Benaiah, David descended from the crest of Olivet on the way down to the Jordan. As long as he kept a steady pace, the lion claws hovered, but did not grab. Still, the pain haunted his body, and dulled his mind. It was enough to put one foot ahead of the other. Let Joab and Benaiah fret about the future.

Coming toward them from a side path, some farmers were leading two heavily laden asses as if they were coming to market. David had a sour thought: perhaps they'd be asking a king's ransom to provision the fugitive troops. Pain made him vicious. He'd have the farmers cut down, and take the provisions.

But as the farmers drew nearer, David recognized Ziba, servant to Mephibosheth. He felt a happy relief; he'd have news of Jonathan's son. Perhaps Ziba would tell him that Mephibosheth had escaped the city and was on his way to join him. He could share his aches and pains with the youth who understood them; in his exile, he would have a vestige of Jonathan.

Ziba came before him and made a groveling bow. "May the Lord bless you, O King." He gestured toward the asses. "You see, I have brought provisions for Your Majesty."

"I am grateful to you, Ziba."

"Provisions to keep you strong . . . yes, strong . . . while the dogs of Absalom hold the city."

"You are loyal."

"Oh, yes . . . yes . . . to the Lord's anointed." And he put a fidgeting hand on the load one of the asses carried. "Two hundred loaves of bread—the finest—I have brought."

"What news do you have of Mephibosheth?"

Ziba licked his lips and gestured to the second ass. "A hundred clusters of raisins, made from the sweetest grapes."

David stared at the jumpy little man. "Ziba. Is Mephibosheth well?"

Ziba's eyes scurried like mice. "A hundred bunches of summer fruit . . . and, yes . . . over here, a flagon of wine . . ."

David's voice was imperious. "Answer my question, Ziba. Where is Mephibosheth?"

"He is in Jerusalem, my Lord. He stays in Jerusalem."

"Why?"

Ziba tugged at his robe. His eyes were downcast. "It is understandable. He is young. And you have left the city. . . ."

"What are you trying to tell me, Ziba?"

The words tumbled out of Ziba's mouth. "I am loyal, my Lord. See, I have come to you out of Jerusalem, and I have

54

brought bread and raisins and wine and summer fruit and two fine asses for Your Majesty to ride upon."

David grabbed Ziba by the collar of his robe, and held tight, the pain wrenching his back; his breathing was labored. "Tell me . . . why Mephibosheth stays in Jerusalem."

"He thinks . . . yes . . . it is that he thinks . . . that the Israelites might restore him to his grandfather's throne."

David's hand dropped to his side. He frowned. The Evil Spirit churned within him like bile. He looked at Ziba and the laden asses. "You are loyal, Ziba. You shall be rewarded." He turned to Joab. "Witness what I say. I gave the estates of Saul to Mephibosheth out of my love for Jonathan and loyalty to the pledge we made to each other in the name of the Lord, between him and me and between his children and mine. But I have been betrayed. Now I give the estates of Saul, and all else that belongs to Mephibosheth, to Ziba."

Ziba's eyes glistened as he bowed. "I am your humble servant, sir; may I continue to stand well with you."

But Joab snorted.

FOUR

The gates of Jerusalem stood open, a hole in the wall that protected the north side of the city. The people who had stayed behind when David left stood about the streets in the noon sun, gathered in clusters, talking in low voices.

On the western hill, the troops of Absalom were clearly visible, the tents, the moving figures, the glint of sword, spear and armor in the sunlight. But Jerusalem itself seemed hushed and almost empty. It lay in the heat, awaiting Absalom's will.

At the House of Cedar, Michal sat in her chambers. She traced in her mind the journey that her male slave had made to Paltiel in Ephraim. He would have arrived the previous nightfall. Paltiel, if he had set out at daybreak, would be nearing Jerusalem now. Or would he be coming at all? Perhaps, now that she had been the property of the King, he didn't want her anymore.

At the thought, she felt old and tired. Her life at Absalom's court would be even worse than it had been at David's; he would have no need of her to sanctify his conquest. He was heir to David's throne, and David had fled in defeat. Even her presence was useless.

Paltiel . . . Paltiel . . . come to me!

* ❀ ❀

Mephibosheth lay on his pallet, pain still throbbing in his feet. He concentrated on the pain, letting it befog the thoughts and images that passed across his mind. He did not want to think of Absalom, but the face of Absalom imposed itself on a whole bestiary in his imagination. The face of Absalom on a lion. The face of Absalom on a serpent. The face of Absalom on a wheeling hawk. Even the face of Absalom glowing, disembodied, in a midnight darkness, damp with the vapors of the spirit world.

That morning he had called in a maidservant and asked for Ziba. But the maidservant had told him that Ziba was nowhere about. Where was he? She did not know; she only knew that he had left the city the night before in haste. Mephibosheth had felt sickened. He could visualize Ziba passing through the north gate to seek out Absalom, bowing and scraping to make his peace and gain some favor from the New Anointed. Perhaps Ziba had brought an offering, some choice grains or livestock from Mephibosheth's own lands! Mephibosheth recoiled. He'd have sent Absalom a sack of manure. But Ziba was always politic. Mephibosheth wearied of his oily ways, but he knew that Ziba had saved him many a penalty his impetuosities had earned.

The maidservant entered. "My Lord, Hushai is here. He comes from Olivet, and he wishes to see you."

"Hushai?" Mephibosheth raised himself on one elbow. "*Hushai?*"

"Yes, my Lord."

"But he is with David!"

"He is here."

Mephibosheth felt puzzled and anxious. "Help me to my feet and get my tunic."

Dressed, Mephibosheth eased himself into a chair. "You may send Hushai in now."

Hushai bowed. "King David inquired after you, and I told him I would find how it goes with you."

"How should I know? We wait for Absalom."

"Indeed. Quite so."

"The city is sealed off now. Why are you here?"

Hushai hesitated. When he spoke, his voice was leaden. "I came back from Olivet to offer my humble services to the new King."

"You left David . . . to come to Absalom?"

Hushai paused again. "Yes."

Rage propelled Mephibosheth to his feet. He stood, swaying and trembling. "I was trampled by guards, cried out for a litter or an ass, had my crippleness ground into my soul by Ziba . . . to try to go to David for the same love for him I thought you had. And you have *left* him? There in in the desert? Defeated? You *left* him? What serpent eats your vitals, Hushai? What buzzard in you is drawn to the carrion of Absalom?"

Hushai's eyes, so bland, so hooded, suddenly flashed. "You cloak yourself in Jonathan's arrogance, Mephibosheth. You think you can possess David as wholly in your weakness as Jonathan possessed him in his strength. No other love so strong. No other loyalty so perfect. You live a legend, Mephibosheth. But Absalom is real. He stands outside those gates, and he will take the city. No sweet memories you conjure will stop him, nor can you hobble to any rescue. So don't rant at me of loyalty. I will do what I will do, nor will I ever trust you with my purposes! Stay with your legend, Mephibosheth. It's all you have."

And Hushai left the room.

Mephibosheth lurched to his pallet and flung himself upon it.

The ram's horns sounded. The Canaanite girls, clad in garlands of flowers, danced through the gates of Jerusalem. Their bare breasts and loins gleamed sweet as the flowers that colored their bodies, pinks and yellows and azures and violets. Over their heads, they carried clay images of Astarte, and chanted their homage to the goddess, beating the air with the flutter of their song.

Plodding troops followed. Men of Asher, and Zebulun, Issachar and Naphtali; men of Manasseh and Dan. They marched with even stride, their eyes straight ahead. They did not seem to be victorious troops, more like military workmen, determined to do what they felt had to be done. They were asserting Israel among the tribes of Jacob; the north country had never received any special favor of King David. Under Absalom, they felt, matters would change. After all, Absalom's grandfather, Talmai, Prince of Geshur, led the Geshurites through the gates into Jerusalem. Blood counted in statecraft.

On the streets beside the marching troops, the people who had stayed in Jerusalem had gathered. Some cheered. Most stared impassively as the troops went by. King David's flight was no cause of special celebration; it was more like a death in the family. Perhaps it was inevitable; but it was sad.

The mood of the crowd changed when three snorting horses came through the gate, each crowned with a feathered headdress and decked with silver harnessing. They drew a Cretan chariot on which Absalom stood, cracking a whip over the horses as if he drove all the Cretan and Pelethite hosts before him. His hair, falling to his shoulders, was held in place by a gold headband. Gold bracelets gleamed on his arms. His tunic, of white linen, was embroidered with silver thread that shimmered in the sunlight. His chariot was surrounded by Canaanite girls who tossed flowers at the crowd along the street. Boys in loincloths carried bowls of burning incense that filled the air with exotic fumes. Behind the chariot, musicians played on horn and flute, drum and finger cymbals. And above it all, Absalom held his whip in one hand and stretched his other arm in gracious gestures to the crowd, which cheered the regal display. No such celebration had been seen in the town since David had brought the Ark to Jerusalem.

Behind the musicians, riding on asses, were Absalom's courtiers and counselors, led by the sleepy-eyed Ahithophel, who watched the crowd with casual disdain. Then came the troops of Judah and Simeon, lately come from Hebron as escort to Absalom. They brought a special sanctity; David had first been anointed King in Hebron.

Absalom drew his horses to a halt before the Tabernacle in the center of the city. He stepped to the ground and passed the stone altar that stood before the entry to the Tabernacle. Zadok and Abiathar, chief priests, stood on either side of the tentlike structure and bowed as Absalom approached. Absalom hesitated for a moment, looking from one priest to the other, trying to catch some hint of what he might find within. But the faces of the priests were as blank as stone.

Absalom drew aside the curtain. Lowering his head, he drew aside the veil. There, before him, defined by glints of gold, was the Ark. David had left it in Jerusalem. Absalom stood gazing in wonderment. The Ark belonged not in a place, but with a person—the King, the embodiment of the tribes of Jacob. So it had been with Saul. So it had been with David. The Ark went with the King into battle, as a sign of the Will of the Lord. But David had fled. The Ark remained. Absalom stood in the Presence, and he felt, as he had never felt before, a great fear. Could he truly be King as David had been King? Looking at the Ark, all Absalom's fantasies of power, all he had plotted to achieve, were suddenly stripped, naked and defenseless before that Awesome Thing that confronted him in the silent darkness of the Tabernacle. God's judgment? He knew that mystical tradition. But there was little mysticism in Absalom's awe. What he confronted, left behind in Jerusalem, was his father's judgment. The Ark was as real as his father's eyes.

He wavered, then straightened. He let the veil fall, pushed aside the curtain, and emerged into the sunlight. He turned to Zadok and Abiathar. "I will make a burnt offering to the Lord."

With Ahithophel close beside him, Absalom watched in silent piety while the priests performed the rite on the stone altar and saw the clouds of smoke ascend to the sky. He wondered if the smoke were visible on Olivet. Would his father know that he was enjoining the Lord's help for his own kingship? Would he rage? Would he plot battle? Or would he be resigned and vanish into Gilead? Even so, would Absalom's throne ever be safe as long as the old man lived? Though he tended flocks in the most distant desert, he was still David.

The ritual ended, Absalom looked sharply at the priests, trying to detect some response in their eyes—some look of approval, or submission, or hostility that might guide him in his dealings with them. But they were impassive. He wondered about them. Perhaps he would have to replace them with others loyal to him. That might be politically difficult. And it would strengthen his court if the chief priests of his father's reign also served under his reign. He would let the matter pass . . . for now.

He turned from the Tabernacle and faced, across an open square, the House of Cedar, the dark brown of its great facade contrasting with the sandy earth of the roads and the mud-brick of the other buildings. It loomed with the majesty of its Phoenician design, strange carvings on its planes and columns. The eaves of its roof overhung and shadowed its latticed windows. Who watched behind them? What danger had David left behind to strike from curtained rooms or ambush in the turn of a corridor?

Absalom, his hand on his sword hilt, started to walk toward the great door, but Ahithophel put a hand on his arm. "You should be preceded by guards, my Lord." He gestured to Talmai of Geshur, Absalom's grandfather, standing close by. "Perhaps your men of Geshur might lead the way into the House of Cedar."

Talmai gave a wry smile. "I would have dreamed of ushering Absalom to David's throne. I will do it now in memory of Tamar."

Ahithophel and Absalom nodded solemnly and for a moment, tears shone in Absalom's eyes. He blinked them away quickly.

Talmai hailed his men. In tight formation, they marched toward the great door. They drew their swords, pushed the doors open, and disappeared into cavernous darkness. Absalom and Ahithophel followed.

To Absalom it was like entering a spirit world, filled with presences that lurked in the darkness and flicker of lamplight. There, the figure of his father, robed as a patriarch. Beyond, his mother, Maacah, beckoning to him. He heard his sister Tamar, moaning behind a curtain, and thought he saw in the shadows the hunched form of Mephibosheth, hobbling. He had his sword half-drawn at a vision of Amnon that was, at another moment, a column of wood.

He felt Ahithophel's hand on his arm again and jumped at the touch. But Ahithophel's voice was even and low. "My Lord, calm yourself. This is your moment of triumph."

In the wake of the Geshurite troops, a strange pair slipped into the House of Cedar. One was a young man, dressed in the short tunic of a court slave with a chain bracelet welded on his arm. The other was a middle-aged man with a close-cropped, graying beard and a steady eye. But his hair was disheveled and he wore the rags of a beggar, mottled and covered with dirt.

While the soldiers of Geshur thumped through the corridors, their swords drawn, the young man led his companion, gliding through curtains and back passageways, deep into the House of Cedar until they came to a certain doorway. He bowed to the beggarman, drew open a curtain, and said, "I will wait here."

The beggarman passed through the doorway.

Michal screamed at the intrusion of this beggar in her chambers. Then, as suddenly as she had screamed, she put her hand across her mouth. The figure before her stood erect and his eyes grew visible in the lamplight. Michal screamed again and threw herself into the beggar's arms.

"Paltiel! What's happened to you?"

Paltiel brushed a few smudges of dirt off his robe, and grinned. "Who would bother an old beggarman on a great day like this?"

Michal stood back in her robe of white linen, bordered with Tyrian purple. "Where did you get those clothes, out of the goat pen?"

Paltiel examined his rags fastidiously. "I think some of them were used to bed down newborn calves." He held up a frayed tatter. "They are rather convincing."

"My dear." She laughed as the tears ran down her cheeks. "I'd give you my last shekel."

"No need." He looked at her with his steady eyes. "All I want is my wife."

"Take me, Paltiel." She was in his arms again, pressed against the rags. "Take me. . . ."

Three beggars passed out of the House of Cedar—an older man, a woman, and a young man. They made their way through Jerusalem to the north gate, headed for a farm in Ephraim. In the excitement of Absalom's arrival, no one noticed.

Absalom stood at the entry of the room, Ahithophel on one side of him, Talmai on the other. He felt an awe almost as great as he had felt in the Tabernacle. The room was large, the floor covered with thick carpets. On the walls were richly sewn hangings. Here and there were low tables and thick leather cushions. Sunlight shone through the latticed windows, making strange figures on the ornate weave of the carpets. But one object, directly across from the entry, dominated all else. It was a massive chair of carved wood. Absalom knew the chair. It had been Saul's chair. It had been Ishbosheth's chair when he was King of Israel. Moved to Jerusalem, it had been David's chair when he ruled all the tribes of Jacob. Now it stood empty in the big room. Saul had been killed at Gilboa; Ishbosheth was beheaded; David had fled. Now Ahithophel and Talmai ushered Absalom to the chair.

"It is your rightful place, Absalom," Ahithophel said softly, and gestured for him to be seated.

Absalom recoiled, as if the great arms of the chair would close about him and crush him. He glanced at Ahithophel, then at Talmai. Their eyes were filled with pride as they waited. He counted them as friends. But might they be his executioners?

He looked about the room as if to find some escape and caught sight of a circle of polished silver set in one of the hangings near the throne. In the silver he saw his own image—the long hair, the gold headband, the proud face with the heavy brow, regal in its strength. He pictured that image with the multitudes bowed before it, and felt a surge of excitement. No one would oppose so kingly a presence, plot against so magnificent a bearing. He . . . *he* would be safe on the throne.

Slowly he took his seat, pressed his back against the heavy wood, ran his hands over the polished arms, and looked at Ahithophel. "What is the business of the court?"

Ahithophel spoke deliberately. "Perhaps it would be best if we first found out what is left of David's court here in the House of Cedar."

Absalom nodded.

Talmai said, "We know the concubines are still here. Ten of them."

"I knew your soldiers would find them out," said Absalom. "Who else?"

Talmai frowned. "Mephibosheth, son of Jonathan."

"So . . . my father left me that crippled baggage." Absalom stared across the room. "Strange. All he had left of . . . sweet Jonathan. I'll deal with him later. Who else?"

"That's all we've found so far, except for servants and slaves."

"Do one more search," Absalom said. "Michal might be here. She lost no love on David, and she might be . . . useful."

Talmai left to round up his men for the search.

Ahithophel grew more sleepy-eyed than ever. "Let us think, Absalom, of your father's concubines . . ."

"You think of them. I have my own."

Ahithophel held up his hand. "No . . . no . . . attend me a moment. Israel needs to be assured of your resolve if you are to ask of them their loyalty."

"*My* resolve! What more? I have taken Jerusalem. I have sacrificed before the Ark. I sit on David's throne. What more do they need of my resolve?"

"But you are David's son. And David is still alive. Suppose he returns, and your heart surges with filial piety. If you let *him* sit on the throne, what will he do to those who have rebelled against him?"

"Ahithophel, you conjure fantasies!"

"Fantasies sometimes rule men."

"All right!" Absalom glowered at Ahithophel. "Give me your advice. How should I act?"

"I suggest you have intercourse with your father's concubines . . . in public."

"*What?*"

"Purely as a matter of politics."

"Politics?"

"Indeed. Then all Israel will know that you have given great offense to your father. This will confirm the resolution of your followers."

Absalom stared at his counselor, and a slow smile came across his face. "Ahithophel, you have a certain mad wisdom."

Ahithophel bowed. "Thank you, my Lord."

"But from what I have seen of my father's concubines, this will truly be a sacrifice for Israel."

Ahithophel's hand gestured vaguely. "But . . . even going through the motions . . ."

"Do not worry. I shall be brave."

65

Talmai reentered the royal audience room with some Geshurite soldiers. "My Lord, there is no sign of Michal; her chambers are empty. But we have found . . . and this is puzzling . . . Hushai, the Archite."

"Hushai?" Absalom glanced at Ahithophel, whose face had suddenly clouded. "Puzzling indeed. Send him in."

Everyone in the room was watchful as Hushai entered. Absalom remembered him as one of David's closest advisers, as respected as Ahithophel. But Hushai had stayed in David's court while Ahithophel had come to Absalom in Hebron. Where did Hushai stand now? Was he a spy, left behind by David, or did his wisdom now lead him to believe that the power had indeed passed from David's hands?

Hushai bowed low. "Long live the King."

No one spoke.

Hushai repeated. "Long live the King."

"Is this your loyalty to your friend?" Absalom's voice was harsh. "Why did you not go with David?"

"Because I mean to attach myself to the man chosen by the Lord, and by the people of Israel, and with him I will remain. Whom ought I to serve? Should I not serve the son? I will serve you as I have served your father."

Hushai's words were smoothly spoken, almost as if he had memorized them, but they had eloquence, Absalom looked at Ahithophel, who was stone-faced, but then, perhaps Ahithophel was jealous of another counselor with whom he might have to share the ear of the King. He looked at Talmai, his grandfather and a shrewd judge of men. Their eyes met. Talmai nodded. He was evidently impressed. Absalom, himself, basked in the words "I will serve you as I have served your father." With Ahithophel and Hushai, both, Absalom would have inherited great wisdom from David's court. With both to counsel him, he would be able to counter any moves that David might make; they would know how David thought, and how he might act.

Absalom made his decision. "You may stay in my court, Hushai, as counselor to the King."

66

❈ ❈ ❈

Later that afternoon, blasts of ram's horns called Absalom's followers to the square before the House of Cedar. On the flat roof of the house, close to the edge and visible to all, a tent had been put up. Beneath the canopy lay a pallet covered with fine linen. Absalom, clad in his tunic, appeared beneath the canopy. Facing the crowd in the square, and raising his arms high above his head, he shouted, "Let all Israel know who is King. Let all Israel know how the King takes his pleasures!"

And the first concubine was led to him by a male slave. Ahithophel had told him, "You must take them in order of precedence. The concubines are each very conscious of their order in the scheme of things."

"Am I to take all ten?" Absalom had asked anxiously.

"Three, I think, will be sufficient," Ahithophel had replied. "The chief concubine and her two eldest sisters."

"Why not the youngest?"

"That would violate precedence."

"Oh," said Absalom, and consoled himself with the thought that there would be time enough for the rest.

Now he was confronted with the chief concubine. Plump, frizzy-haired, with a face ravaged by the years, she smiled at Absalom in anticipation. But Absalom, his ardor drained, concluded that his father had found her before the Flood. Still, he knew what kingship demanded.

With elaborate gestures, he displayed the concubine to the crowd below like a pearl of Egypt, loosened her gown, and let it fall. At the sight of her ample flesh, the crowd cheered. Absalom eased her to the pallet, where she lay in mounds.

Turning to the crowd again, Absalom rubbed his crotch as if to suggest a rage of stiffened desire, but he was very careful not to display the shriveled reality.

He put himself down upon her, raising his tunic as he did so to let the crowd admire the royal buttocks that would weight a demonic thrusting.

67

Knowing that he had nothing to thrust with, Absalom started a slow rhythm with his buttocks while the concubine eyed him with disappointed confusion. He let the rhythm quicken as the crowd, in its ignorance, cheered each imagined plunge, until, with a great contortion, Absalom cried out a paean of ecstasy. And the crowd answered with an empathetic sigh.

Absalom, straighteninig his tunic, helped the concubine to her feet and put her gown about her with courtly movements. He watched, with gratitude, as the slave led her away. But his ordeal had just begun.

Next came a rail of a woman who might have been young in Abraham's time. By now the crowd, fancying itself a partner to Absalom's lust, would have cheered the Witch of En-dor. As he let the gown fall from her, Absalom averted his eyes to spare himself the cadaverous spectacle, but the crowd was noisy with enthusiasm as he laid her upon the pallet. He felt arms and legs entwine him, clutching, as he attempted a new pantomime of ravishment, his eyes closed against the stark reality. Again, with writhing hips, he simulated a climax of wild abandon and hastily stood up so that the concubine could be led away.

He wondered, in despair, why his father had not mummified his senior concubines in the Egyptian manner and set them about the House of Cedar as nostalgic decoration.

Still a third concubine was presented to him, but by now Absalom was numb and went through the motions as if he played through a nightmare. The goading crowd flayed him with its vicarious spasms of groanings and grunts as Absalom finished the grotesquerie and got to his feet, flushed and sweating.

He faced the crowd and raised his arms again in what seemed to be triumph. But within, he struggled with nausea. Amid the cheering, Absalom retired. On the way to the audience chamber, he met Ahithophel, whose sleepy eyes seemed to glow with satisfaction. "A great performance, my

Lord. Your followers are pledged to you." Absalom glowered at him, and went on into the audience chamber.

Before the evening meal, Absalom called together the counselors and tribal elders to consult with them on what action should be taken about David and the remnants of his troops. He deeply hoped that no mention would be made of the rooftop fiasco that aftenoon, but as elder after elder came before him, there was approving talk of "a bold stroke," "a daring move," and even some less sober remarks about the attributes of various of the concubines. At a distance, apparently, some of them had looked attractive.

Absalom dismissed the talk summarily, with a few pungent glances at Ahithophel. But Ahithophel seemed undisturbed; he had heard the comments from the tribal elders, which made Absalom all the more disgruntled.

Absalom opened the meeting brusquely. David by now had probably passed over Olivet with his followers on the way to the Jordan. If he got to the other side of the river, he might be able to recruit friendly troops and regroup. On the other hand, the troops now in Jerusalem were tired after long marches and could use rest before setting out to pursue David's forces. What advice had the elders and counselors to offer?

Some of the elders from the north felt that, once Jerusalem had been taken, the men of the northern tribes would just as soon enjoy their triumph for a while before setting out on a campaign to try to destroy David's troops. Talmai agreed. "They won't take kindly to the desert after the sweetness of Jerusalem."

But Ahithophel struck like a serpent. "Let me pick a thousand men, and I will pursue David tonight. I will overtake him when he is tired and dispirited. I will cut him off from his people and they will all scatter; and I will kill no one but David."

There was silence in the room. David's ghostly presence—so many had seen him only here in the audience chamber—was palpable. Now Ahithophel would kill the King; loyalties would be sundered. Israel might be rent with the anarchy that had existed before Saul. Ahithophel seemed to sense the fear. He talked on, his voice conciliatory.

"I will bring all the people over to you as a bride is brought to her husband. It is only one man's life you are seeking; the rest of them will be unharmed."

Absalom stirred uneasily in his chair. "One man's life." He had felt rage at that "one man." Even now the embers of that rage were still hot. But Ahithophel had evoked a vision of a sword poised against his father's throat, the burst of blood, the twist of the body as the life drained out. He looked about the room, all eyes focused on him. One word, one gesture from him, and Ahithophel would have his way. But Absalom was still, looking from face to face. His eyes rested on Hushai.

"Shall we do what he says?" Absalom asked. "If not, say what you think."

Hushai shook his head. "David is a hardened warrior and savage as a bear in the wilds, robbed of her cubs. So are the men with him."

Absalom noticed the elders of Judah nodding in agreement.

"Your father is an old campaigner and will not spend the night with the main body; even now he will be lying in a pit or some other place. If you attack the main body of his troops, and any of your men are killed at the onset, anyone who hears the news will say, 'Disaster has overtaken the followers of Absalom.' The courage of the most resolute and lionhearted will melt away, for all Israel knows that your father is a man of war and has determined men with him."

Again, the elders of Judah assented, and even some of the elders of the northern tribes grew restive.

"So . . . what is your advice, Hushai?"

"Simply this." Hushai's voice grew stronger and more self-assured. "Wait until the whole of Israel, from Dan to Beer-sheba, is gathered about you, and you shall march with them in person. Then we shall come upon him somewhere, wherever he may be, and descend on him like dew falling on the ground, and not a man of his family or followers will be left alive."

Absalom looked again from face to face and saw the agreement he wanted to see. He measured his words. "Hushai, the Archite, gives us better advice than Ahithophel."

Hushai bowed.

Ahithophel left the room.

Absalom felt relieved. Time enough now, he thought, to enjoy his own special sweetness of Jerusalem.

Late that evening, Absalom stood naked in the royal chambers while Elon, his youthful armor-bearer, washed his body with heated water and soft linen. The lamps around the room cast a gentle light that caught the wisps of incense smoke which curled as it rose. Absalom felt a languor permeate his body as the linen coursed over his torso and loins. It eased his nagging doubts.

Perhaps Ahithophel had been right. Perhaps it would have been wiser to have dealt with David quickly while he was still reeling in flight. But then again, as Hushai had pointed out, David was a hardened warrior. Maybe the flight was a ruse. Maybe David was using himself as bait to lure Absalom's troops into some murderous ambush. But David was getting old. Perhaps the sight of all those troops assembled on the western hill had led to nothing but panic. Once the panic passed, the opportunity that Ahithophel wanted him to grasp would be gone forever.

Whatever. The decision had been made. Nothing could be gained by poking around among dead possibilities. He would celebrate Jerusalem, and settle, at least, one old score. Mephibosheth was in the House of Cedar and, in his own good time, Absalom was going to find him.

Once Elon had dried Absalom's body, he brought in a tray covered with cruets of fragrant oils.

"Where did you find these?" Absalom asked.

"They are from David's private stores."

A faint smile crossed Absalom's face. "Use them liberally."

Elon gave just the trace of an answering smile. "Yes, my Lord."

With practiced hands, Elon applied the oils to Absalom's neck and shoulders. "Your muscles are still tense, my Lord."

"Not surprising for this day."

"I can tell you now," Elon said. "I never thought it would happen."

"You had little faith, young one."

"But it seemed so great a thing. Jerusalem. The King."

"My father. His mind as hateful, sometimes, and his judgment as clouded as any man's." His voice was suddenly bitter. "I knew that hatefulness. He vented it on me. For five long years he vented it on me."

"I'm sorry I spoke. Your muscles grow tighter than ever."

"They will begin to loosen . . . now. David's oils are soothing." And he let Elon's hands nurture his languor.

He picked up a mirror of polished silver and viewed his own face, his glistening torso. The splendor of it, as he admired it, seemed quite apart from himself. He was only gifted with this vehicle for his spirit. Still, his spirit was warmed by the wonder that, even that afternoon on the rooftop, the splendor had evoked in the crowds of his followers. Truly it was a king's body, and the royal chambers its fitting habitat.

But as he looked in the mirror, he sensed a ghostly shadow image—Amnon. The indolent eyes. The slack jaw. The pouchy cheeks. He felt, even now with Amnon long since killed, a wave of revulsion. It might have been Amnon, the eldest of David's sons, heir to David's throne, who looked into this mirror.

Then what was Absalom's image? He had heard it said: Absalom, murderer and usurper. And he had raged at the accusation. He had been the first to see his sister Tamar after Amnon, her half-brother, had raped her. She had come to

Absalom's house hysterical, ashes on her head, her robe rent, sobbing uncontrollably. He had held her, tried to quiet her, sought to find out what had happened, but the sobbing had gone on for an hour or more before she could get the words out—how Amnon had feigned illness, how David had sent her to care for him, how Amnon had forced himself on her, and then, in sudden hatred, had her thrown out of the house.

Absalom had cloistered her in his own house, and had gone to Maacah, David's wife and his and Tamar's mother, and told her what had happened. Would she tell David, or would he? Maacah had wrung her hands helplessly. Ahinoam and her son Amnon were much favored by the King, more so than she. If she went to David, would he not think she was just trying to stir up mischief with some idle gossip to bring sympathy for her own children?

Absalom had been sickened by his mother's hesitancy, and had gone and told David himself, thinking that, in common justice, punishment would come swiftly to Amnon. David had stormed about the room after hearing what Absalom told him. Absalom waited for punishment to come to Amnon, and waited, and waited, while he saw his sister, at his own house, grow wan and sometimes distraught, despairing of ever marrying, despairing of her own life.

But Amnon continued in attendance at the House of Cedar, serene, oblivious, unpunished, and seemingly as much in David's favor as ever. The very sight of him was gall to Absalom, the more so as his sister's health grew poorer. And he felt himself and his mother Maacah on the very edges of the court while Amnon enjoyed the perogatives of a prince.

Absalom had held his peace and his temper for two years, waiting for David's justice. But no justice came from the King. Finally, after seeing Tamar weakening, Absalom held a sheep-shearing on his lands in Baal-hazor, invited Amnon, and prepared him a feast fit for a king. When Amnon was merry with wine, Absalom had him stabbed to death by the servants. Taking Tamar with him, Absalom had fled to his grandfather, Talmai, in the north country of Geshur. He stayed there three years before David allowed him to return to Jerusalem, but without Tamar, who was too sick to travel. He stayed in Jerusalem another two years before David granted him an audience and welcomed him back to the court at the House of Cedar. He was heir to the throne, but he was a stranger. The one who sat close to David, the one on whom David lavished his favor, as he had on Amnon, was Mephibosheth.

The odors of David's oils were heavy in the warm room. Absalom inhaled them deeply as he felt Elon's hands knead the muscles of his shoulders. Finally Elon asked, "Shall I comb your hair now, my Lord?"

Absalom hesitated, then crossed the room to a raised couch and lay on it full-length, still naked, his body gleaming with the oils, his hair falling from the top end of the couch. "No." He gestured to Elon to draw close and spoke to him in a conspiratorial whisper. "Attend me, Elon. Go to the concubine quarters. Select the one *lowest* in precedence, the youngest and the prettiest. Send her here to me."

"Yes, my Lord."

"And take one for yourself, if you've a mind. Just avoid the chief concubine." He closed his eyes and ran his hand across his forehead. "I've tried her."

Elon smiled. "Thank you, my Lord." And he disappeared.

Absalom reached over and took up one of the oil cruets, turning it slowly in the light, admiring the scarlets and ambers, the murky blues and greens. Glass. Egyptian perhaps, or maybe Phoenician. He would have to learn about these graceful royal things, so far from Geshur. He would surround himself with beauty. David had spoken so often of the time he had spent in Philistine Gath as guest of King Achish. He had described the marbles and fine woods, the strange sculptures and mosaics.

Absalom had visions of plundering the south and bringing all that beauty to Jerusalem. He had no intentions of reigning over a nation of wheat farmers and sheepherders. At times he felt that David had never really left the hills of Judea and his flocks there. Jerusalem was still as dusty as the desert. In Absalom's reign, there would be grandeur in Jerusalem.

He did not hear the concubine enter. In the course of his ruminations, he simply noticed her standing there beside the couch, her eyes downcast as if she shielded them against the gleam of Absalom's body. She was a slight girl with dark skin and a catlike Egyptian grace. Amalekite, probably. Some of David's more recent loot. He was grateful that at least one of David's stable of whores could titillate him.

He raised her chin with his finger until she looked him in the face. Her eyes were large, liquid, and fearful. Absalom liked that. Fear bred exquisite submissions. "What is your name?"

"Yafa."

"You are from the south?"

"I was captured near the River of Egypt when I was a child."

He thought her barely more than a child now. "Do you like my body?"

"I . . . I dare not look at it."

"Oh, but you will, child, you will." He tilted her chin so that her eyes looked the length of him to his feet. Then he handed her his gold comb. "You may comb my hair."

She moved to the head of the couch, her light tunic close over the budding of her body. He felt a gentle pressure of the comb on his hair. Her very touch, he thought, would add to its youthful luster.

"I understand that Mephibosheth remains in the House of Cedar."

"Yes, my Lord."

"He awaits me?"

"He stays in his quarters. We have brought him food, but he does not eat."

"He communes, perhaps, with God?"

"We do not know his spirit."

Absalom stared at the room's ceiling. "I shall find it."

He relaxed in the steady rhythm of the concubine's

combing as he brooded about Mephibosheth. Why had he stayed? Did he think that he, with those big doe-eyes and grotesque hobble, could wrest the kingship from Absalom and take it for the house of Saul? Ridiculous! Mephibosheth was only fit to be the king of the fools.

Still, there was blood in him. The blood of Jonathan and Saul. Fierce blood, however weakly it drooled through his veins. Perhaps in the turmoil of Absalom's ascension, his blood would quicken and those doe-eyes harden with aspiration. Improbable. But possible.

Kill him? Or humble him? Absalom relished the image of his royal progress decorated by a sycophant grandson of Saul. In Mephibosheth's person as courtier, Absalom would have further legitimacy, stretching all the way back to Samuel's anointment of his grandfather. Absalom would then be at the apex of royalty—David vanquished, Mephibosheth abased. Yes, better to humble him. Time enough later to kill him.

Absalom stirred on his couch. "You have combed enough. Come. Stand beside me."

She moved and stood close to his flank.

"Hand me my silver mirror."

"Yes, my Lord." And she put it in his hand.

Rising on one elbow, Absalom examined his hair as it fell in cascades about his shoulders. "Yes. Better, even, than Elon. You shall be my hair-comber."

"I am your servant for whatever you desire."

"So you are." He gazed at her intently, and wondered what pleasure David had had with her and how she had coped with the fumblings of an old man. She would find matters different with him; he would let her climb his mountainous passions . . . gradually. "Now, then, Yafa, you may touch my private parts."

She looked at him questioningly and then moved to bow her head over his groin.

"No. No. Just with your hand. With your hand, only."

Yafa straightened and slowly put out her hand until it rested on Absalom's flesh. Her eyes were no longer downcast

76

but focused on her hand, and the flesh beneath. Her hand closed with childlike hesitancy, as if she cherished a sea creature that quivered in her palm.

Absalom stretched out on the couch, his head flung back, his eyes closed, and let her gossamer touch permeate his whole body. His flesh hardened.

"It is enough," he told her, and eased her hand away.

She looked at him, puzzled. "Do I not please you?"

"I wish only to be aroused." He raised himself from the couch. "Now, my robe. The red one."

"Do you wish your underlinens, first?"

"No. Only my robe."

She brought it to him, a swath of crimson like the fires of the rising sun. He draped it carefully around his person.

"Now," he said to her, "guide me to the chambers of Mephibosheth."

He walked the lamplit corridors of the House of Cedar as the girl padded ahead of him, her wisplike figure barely visible in the shadows. Soon she stopped, and pointed to a curtained doorway. She bowed and disappeared.

Absalom drew aside the curtain and entered. A single lamp burned in the silent room. Absalom stood visible in the lamplight and peered into the darkness. "Mephibosheth!" His voice echoed. "Are you not going to welcome your new King?"

Silence.

"You are here," said Absalom. "I can smell the stench."

More silence. Then a stirring somewhere in the darkened recesses of the room.

Absalom deepened his voice. "The King is waiting."

Mephibosheth moved slowly out of the darkness and stood some distance from Absalom. His stance was rigid, almost defiant.

"Come here."

The figure held its ground. "Has David returned?"

"He has fled to Gilead. He will not return. He has left you here, Mephibosheth."

"I *stayed* here."

"Did you, now? To welcome me? How touching!"

"I stayed here so I would not be a burden to him when he goes into battle with you." The doe-eyes seemed to glow in the darkness.

"Battle me? Ha! He will war with all Israel."

"And prevail!" Mephibosheth's voice was shrill.

"You dream, cripple. I am your King, now. Come here, and do homage."

"I am under David's protection . . ."

"Come here."

"No." But he took a few trembling steps forward. "His pledge. His pledge to Jonathan!" The tone was plaintive. "As long as he lives. And he lives."

"In defeat. In Gilead. And you are here, in my kingdom." Absalom loosened his robe, baring his body. "Kneel to your King."

Mephibosheth went rigid. "No!"

"To the royal body. See? No withering or crippling. Perfect. That is why I am King, Mephibosheth." Absalom grabbed Mephibosheth's hair. "And . . . you . . . will . . . kneel." He forced him to his knees, his face inches away from Absalom's stiffened flesh. "There, now. Look on it. The passage for all future kings, strong and thrusting. Forget your envy and do it homage."

Mephibosheth shook his head violently. But Absalom's grip was strong. "Open your mouth."

Mephibosheth clamped his jaws shut.

"What is this sweet innocence?" Absalom purred. "Your father did homage to the line of David. So, it is said, your grandfather gave homage. Now . . . so will you!" He twisted the hair in his grip.

Mephibosheth cried out.

"Open your mouth." Absalom wrenched the hair again.

Tears started to stream down Mephibosheth's face as his body writhed and struggled helplessly.

"Are you afraid you might become pregnant?" Another wrench. "Like Jonathan?"

Mephibosheth screamed with pain, his mouth opening wide.

"Now!" Absalom tilted Mephibosheth's face upward and forward. "Take it!"

Mephibosheth's mouth encompassed the flesh. He gagged and gasped, but the flesh thrust deeper. He gagged again as the fluid spurted down his throat.

Absalom pushed him back, and he fell, crumpled on the floor, retching and vomiting. Between spasms, he gasped, "Kill . . . me . . . now!"

Absalom stood over the figure, gathering his robe around him. "Later. When I have no use for you."

Absalom left Mephibosheth's room, and returned to the royal chambers.

FIVE

As David descended Olivet on his way to the Jordan, it was Ira's turn to give his shoulder and arm to David as he plodded along the pathway, aching at every step. At a turn in the path, they saw the panorama of the Jordan valley, the sprawling river, and the high bluffs of Gilead beyond.

David spoke. "I think of Moses, old and troubled. Perhaps he sat on one of those bluffs with the children of Israel, and pointed across the Jordan to where we stand. 'Canaan, a land flowing with milk and honey.' Oh, yes. So Moses said. The land promised by the Lord God. But did Moses also say it was a land flowing with outraged Canaanites, Egyptian tribute-agents, belligerent Philistines, caravans and bands of brigands . . . and little water?"

"My Lord," said Ira gently, "your pain fills your head with doubts."

"Indeed. Quite unbefitting a king of Israel. Still, Ira, when you think of it, could the Lord God have thought of a worse place to try to settle some wandering desert tribes? In His power, he made the Red Sea to part. Could He not have caused rain to fall on the deserts of Sinai and let the wilderness bloom? It would have suited us. Yes. Our home after captivity. But no, He lured us on with promises. 'A land flowing with milk and honey.' Ira, what we needed was peace, and a land flowing with water. Just water, to nurture the earth. We could have grown our own milk and honey. What have we nurtured this earth with—this earth—now—where we stand?"

"My Lord . . ."

"Answer me!"

"Our labor and our love of God."

"What piety!"

"I am a priest."

David clamped a viselike grip on his arm and painfully leaned down to pick up a handful of dusty earth. He held it in front of Ira's eyes and crumbled it in his fingers. "Milk? No. Honey? No. Sweat? No. Water? No."

"What, then?"

"Blood." He let the earth fall from his hand. "It dries to dust."

Ira stared at David. "You make me fear for you."

David grew weary. "It will pass, Ira. It will pass. Joab will come to me and stir my spirits, and I shall find blood as sweet as milk and honey. Canaanite blood. Philistine blood. Israelite blood. The blood of Judah. The blood of my son, Absalom. Just so it flows. Just so it nurtures the earth. Isn't that the work of a warrior, Ira, to make blood flow in the name of the Lord?"

"You torment yourself, my Lord."

"Yes . . . Perhaps I do. Excusable in the hearing of a priest. But don't let Joab hear of it. We are prisoners, aren't we, of the partisans of our aggression? They nurse on our virility and our treasury, and we grow weak in our wondrous power." David sighed. "I felt so strong, once."

"Your kingship has been the strength of Israel."

"No . . . no . . . But walking these hills, I remember how I was lord of creation with one sling, one stick, and one dog. My subjects? A hundred head of sheep. Did you ever herd sheep, Ira?"

81

"No, my Lord. My father had orchards of figs."

"Too bad. A fig. It grows. It falls. You can hold it in your hand. But a sheep? A very particular animal, a sheep. Subject to sudden and mysterious illuminations, not unlike some of our more mystical priests. You see, Ira, if you had been a sheepherder, you would know how tremulous is our control as lords of creation. There I have the flock, all nicely bunched, quietly grazing on a green-sprouting hillside under the noonday sun. Time enough to play the harp, my dog Samson resting at my feet, and all serenity about me. An idyllic picture, eh? Ha! Zoof! Off he goes, one of the sheep, to drown himself in the Salt Sea or lose himself in the Wilderness of Zin. Whatever. An illumination in his sheep-brain, and the other sheep start to follow. That, Ira, is when a young man grows strong. First, the sling. Then the dog. Then the stick. And the order of creation is restored. Such an exaltation of strength I'd feel, once the flock was bunched again!

"Sometimes it took just the pebbles from the sling, bursting the dust in front of the sheep's nose like some live and dangerous thing. I was good with the sling. Oh yes, very good. And when I'd falter, I'd practice till I could hit within a thumb's width at twenty paces. If I had a sling, I'd show you. As a matter of fact, get me a sling, and I *will* show you!"

"But your back . . ."

"Never mind my back. Get me a sling."

Ira shrugged, left David for a moment, got a sling from one of the guards, and brought it back to the King. David tested it expertly with his hands. "Good. Fresh wool. Always fresh wool; it has a spring to it." He paused for a moment, and a wan grin crossed his face as he looked at Ira. "Yes, you should know. My skill with a sling is legendary. A part of legend. A part of tradition."

"How is that so?"

"You haven't read those scrolls, have you? Well, I have. Sheva, the chief scribe, showed me one. You see, Sheva is

Egyptian, unanointed and absolutely godless. He doesn't believe a word any Hebrew scribe ever wrote. He keeps snooping around in the scrolls when they aren't watching, just to catch them at something outrageous. Scandalous. I should put a stop to it. But he *does* come up with some choice morsels. I can always tell when he's found something. He comes into the audience chamber with this grin on his face—he looks just like a monkey from the upper Nile that I saw one time caged in Gath—and I know he's found something to lighten my day. I'll never forget when he brought me the story of Samson, the worst oaf, drunk, and whoremonger ever spawned by a child of Jacob. Oh-ho, what a tale the scribes made up about him!

"At any rate, Sheva came in one afternoon, that monkey grin all over his face, and I knew he had something very special. He stood before me very straight—he's a little fellow, you know, comes barely to my shoulder—and he asked in that high sing-song voice of his, 'Who killed Goliath?' Goliath? Goliath? Oh, yes, I remembered. A big fellow. A Philistine from Gath. Killed in battle at Gob. Who killed him? It was Elhanan, a brave man from Bethlehem. And so I told Sheva.

"With a flourish, Sheva unrolls the scroll and reads me some wild story about how I killed Goliath with a single pebble from my sling—right in the forehead. Then I cut off Goliath's head and carried it to Jerusalem. Of course, I was a mere lad then and Jerusalem was in the hands of the Jebusites, but it does make a good story, don't you think? Imagine. One stone from my sling, and the monster was felled!"

David sighed. "Oh, let the tradition say that I was just a defeated old king. But through the years it will be known that as a young man, I was master of the sling! Of course Sheva was unkind enough to point out that it never happened. But he missed the point of legend, of tradition. After all, it *might* have happened. See? I'll show you."

David flexed the sling in his hand. Again, grasping Ira's

arm, he leaned down slowly and picked up a small stone, putting it carefully in the pocket of the sling. David pointed ahead of him. "See that big rock over there?"

"Yes."

"Well, imagine that that is Goliath. And that cleft in the rock, up near the top, that is his forehead."

"All right."

"Now. Stand back."

Ira retreated, watching fretfully as the King took a stance and whirled the sling around, high over his head. With a sudden gasp of pain, he let the sling go with one hand, and put the other hand to his side. The stone sailed out of the sling and landed five paces away from the rock.

David stood, his head bowed, the sling-string loose in his hand, breathing heavily. Ira hurried back to him and held his arm. "My Lord, are you all right?"

David looked at him fiercely. "Another stone. Get me another stone!"

"Please, my Lord. You aren't well."

"Another stone!" David pointed to the ground. "That one, over there!"

Ira picked up the stone and handed it to David, who tucked it in the pocket of the sling, his jaw set, his eyes intent on the rock ahead. He took his stance and raised the sling above his head as Joab came stomping up the line. "David! Just . . . what . . . do you think . . . you are doing?"

David lowered the sling and looked at Joab with a petulant defiance. "I am killing Goliath."

Joab grabbed the sling from his hand. "We are on the march to the Jordan, my Lord, and we have no time for children's games. Come." And he took one arm while Ira took the other. David, between them, kept muttering. "It *might* have happened. Yes, it might."

❖   ❖   ❖

84

The path sloped down between two rolling hills on its way to the Jordan. The path was in shadow, but the afternoon sun struck the hills with a golden light. David was plodding along, now aided by Joab and his brother, Abishai, when a rock bounced and rolled across the path in front of them. The three men looked up to the hill above them and saw a figure, hair and beard a matted mass, tunic tattered, hopping up and down and screaming guttural incoherences. Abishai stared at the strange spectacle. "As if we didn't have enough to contend with. Now, a crazy man!"

David asked, "What is he saying?"

"How should I know? The heat's probably fried his head."

"I heard 'blood,'" David said.

The man came closer and pitched another stone. Joab looked at him sharply. "I know that fellow. Shimei, son of Gera. A Benjamite. Close to the house of Saul."

"Shall I go and cut him down?" Abishai asked.

"No," David said. "No. I want to hear what he is saying."

"What does it matter?"

"He rages to my face. I want to know why he rages."

"You do not need to know. He is mad."

David looked at Abishai with baleful eyes. "You could have said that Absalom was mad, and I should not listen. Indeed, I did not listen. Now, I will listen."

Shimei was closer now, and the words pelted down like the stones he threw. "Get out! Get out, bloody man! It's the vengeance of the Lord! You spilled the blood of Saul's house, and stole the throne. Now Absalom will spill your blood. You murderer! You'll get what's coming to you!"

Abishai pulled his sword. "Let me kill him."

David said, "No." The man was grotesque, but the words he spoke seemed like the words of the Lord's judgment. David turned to Abishai. "If my son, my own son, is out to kill me, who can wonder at this Benjamite?"

Abishai put back his sword reluctantly, and the caravan passed on toward the Jordan. But Shimei's words kept beating on David's spirit. He felt as if his whole body were encrusted with blood, and it weighed him down at every step.

Ever since he had come from Bethlehem, months before, David hated the times when Saul would go on campaigns against the Philistines, Ammonites, or Amalekites, leaving him behind with the women and children and a remnant corps of guards. Even Ishbosheth would be gone, along with David's brothers.

David would mope around the encampment, take long walks in the hills, practice his harp, and wait for Saul to return in several days, sometimes as long as a week. As a youth of fifteen, David felt he was capable of going into battle or at least being part of Saul's retinue in the field, but when he asked him, the king just tousled his hair and said that harpists use up stores that are hard to get in the field. So David stayed at Gibeah, missing Saul and the excitement of the court. Michal tried to entice him into games, but he was in no mood for games. He wanted to go to war. He wanted to be with Saul. And David's determination grew.

When Saul returned to Gibeah after some skirmishes with the Ammonites across the Jordan, he was in a glum mood. Israelite losses had been heavy, and the Ammonites had retreated to their walled city of Rabbah relatively unscathed. David heard about this from Ishbosheth who, once he had gotten back to their tent, lay down on his pallet and wouldn't move. Ishbosheth did not like war.

It was late afternoon. A hot wind blew steadily from the deserts to the south, and the fading sun still poured a golden heat on the hills. Saul, David suspected, might be having a headache; it was likely on hot days, and all the more likely because of the Ammonites.

David tuned his harp carefully, and then, with deliberation, took off his tunic and put on a loincloth of linen. He

86

ran his hands over his body. He put dabs of fragrant oils under his arms and between his thighs. He washed his feet in a bowl of water that stood just inside the tent, and put on his sandals. Taking his harp, he went out of the tent, leaving Ishbosheth immobile, and made his way to the royal tent. Somehow—he did not know quite how—he was going to be with Saul the next time Saul went into the field. He knew how Saul looked at him sometimes, the King's eyes combing his body. If there were persuasion there, he would use that persuasion.

He slipped past the guards into the royal tent and made his way quietly to a dark corner where he sat down, watching Saul, deep in talk with some of his commanders. He could not understand much of what the talk was about— only that it had to do with the skirmish with the Ammonites. But Saul's voice grew louder and louder, and at times he pounded on the arm of his chair with his fist. David felt reassured; Saul was going to have a headache. He clutched his harp and waited.

Saul finally exploded with a long string of Canaanite oaths, his eyes bulging, the veins on his neck standing out, and commanded the warriors out of his sight. They retreated from the tent in haste leaving Saul, breathing heavily, sitting in his chair, holding his head in his hand.

David knew his moment.

He rose and quietly made his way to the throne. Without saying a word he sat down on the rug close to Saul's knee. As he began to play the harp, Saul did not raise his head, but his free hand reached out and rested on David's shoulder.

David let the music flow, wafting it around Saul as if he touched him with his hands. His shoulder rested against Saul's knee, and he felt a responding pressure from Saul. He felt excitement in his groin.

Saul's head still rested on his hand, the fingers pushing against the temples as if to crush spirits pounding inside

87

his skull. But his heavy breathing gradually subsided, and his hand on David's shoulder began to tap the beat of the music. David was intent on his harp, only occasionally glancing up at Saul, but once he noticed Saul's eyes were open and looking at him. His eyes were bloodshot, the circles beneath them dark. David sensed the ache of kingship.

"Are you feeling better, my Lord?"

The big man grunted as he shifted his weight in the chair. "Keep playing, boy. I need the solace."

David felt a welling of pride. *The King needs me.* His fingers moved over the harpstrings as lightly as a breeze. But when he came to the end of a song, David stopped playing and stretched back, his head on a leather cushion next to the throne. He looked at Saul. Their eyes met. Then he saw Saul's eyes wander the length of his body stretched before him, clad only in a loincloth. David trusted to its persuasion, but when he spoke, he tried to keep his voice as casual as possible.

"Would it not be well for the King if I were with him in the field to quiet his spirits? Could you not find some use for me?"

Saul rubbed his cheek and smoothed his beard. "Perhaps you are old enough. I will think about it."

David jumped to his feet. "I promise not to eat too much; not in the field."

Saul smiled. "Warriors eat to keep their strength up . . . and they need their strength."

"Could I go into battle? My sling is true. I practice it."

"Yes, I imagine you struck terror into the sheep."

David stood up very straight. "I can strike fear among the Philistines!"

Saul shook his head. "It would be a blessing from the Lord if someone around here could strike fear into the Philistines."

"Let me try . . ."

88

"Go, boy." He made a gesture of dismissal. "I said, I'll think about it."

David left the royal tent, carrying his harp, walking with a spring to his step.

It was known about Gibeah in the next day or two that Saul's armor-bearer, Jehoab, had been promoted to be one of Jonathan's lieutenants, and that Saul's new armor-bearer would be David of Bethlehem.

David tried to wear Saul's helmet at a rakish angle as he trudged along behind the King, but it kept slipping over his nose. He had Saul's shield hitched over one shoulder, but the weight of it pressed the holding thong into his muscles and he had to keep shifting it every twenty paces or so. His own sword hung at his waist, but he also carried the massive metal of Saul's sword, first under one arm, then under the other, and sometimes over his other shoulder where it, too, pressed the muscle. David was not sure that he was cut out to be an armor-bearer.

He hoped for battle, when Saul would have to take his own helmet, shield, and sword. But battle never seemed to come. It was just marching, marching, marching, and David had to take three paces for every two of Saul's.

They were headed west, down the valley of the Sorek toward Beth-shemesh, which had been threatened by a detachment of Philistines, and Saul, to David's despair, was in an energetic mood, striding along with Abner at his side, his eyes slitted against the afternoon sun, his armor glistening. David had carefully polished each plate before the expedition had begun. Having shifted the weight of the armor around in his lap, David had wondered how Saul could move when he was wearing it, let alone bear the weight of his helmet, sword, and shield. But when David had eased Saul into the armor, he seemed to wear it like a tunic of linen. To the young David there was no man mightier than

89

Saul, no head as noble, no body as manly in its sheer power, muscle and bone defined and molded beneath the skin. In armor, he seemed invincible.

Sundown came mercifully. The army encamped beside the Sorek—only a stream, but its water was clear and cool. David bathed his aching muscles in the stream, and hoped for a long battle the following day.

Saul drank a flagon of wine at evening meal while soldiers set up his tent. It was a small, simple field tent, very different from the royal tent at Gibeah, and intended only for Saul and his armor-bearer. Saul's spear was thrust in the ground, just outside the tent, as a sign that it was the royal tent. Inside were two pallets, a lamp, and Saul's water jar. After the evening meal, Saul had some difficulty rising to his feet. But Abner eased him up, and David steered him to the tent, holding an arm around his waist as the King put one foot slowly in front of the other, heaving great sighs as he did so.

Once inside the tent, David managed to keep Saul standing while he undid the armor and eased it off his shoulders. David swayed as he caught the whole weight of it, but he set it down beside Saul's pallet, leaving Saul clad only in a tunic. In the closeness of the tent, David caught the aroma of Saul's sweat, pungent, and to David, strangely exciting. Saul was no longer the man on the throne; Saul was the man in his care.

David guided Saul a step toward the pallet. Saul stared at it at his feet, and then fell upon it in one earth-shaking thump. He lay there, breathing heavily, the sweat still standing out on his forehead.

David filled the water jar from the Sorek, and brought it back to the tent with a linen towel. Soaking the towel, he gently washed the sweat from Saul's face and neck as the big body lay there inert, careful to wipe the dust from the wrinkles on Saul's forehead and around his eyes. Then, moving downward, he undid Saul's sandals, seeing how the

90

leather had ridged the flesh of his ankles. He washed the dust from his feet.

He put a coverlet over Saul's body; the night was getting cool. Then David went to his own pallet, an arm's length from Saul's, and stripped himself of his sword and girdle and tunic. Shutting the tent-flap, David stretched out on his own pallet and pulled the coverlet up to his chin. He wondered for a few moments what all those women and children were doing in Gibeah. And then he decided he didn't care. He was with Saul.

He turned on his side and was almost asleep when the fearsome sound started. He thought of the thunder of God or a charge of Philistine chariots. But rising on one elbow, he discovered it was only Saul, snoring.

What, he wondered, does one do with a king who snores? David tightened his courage, got out of bed, and with a huge effort, rolled Saul over on his side. The snoring stopped. David went to sleep.

The next day David got his fondest wish—a battle—and regretted it.

Saul and his troops caught a small detachment of Philistines by surprise in some hills just west of Beth-shemesh, and fell on them like wolves. The Philistines, their feathered helmets a rainbow of colors in the sunlight, drew themselves into a circle and fought off the Hebrews with iron-tipped spears and iron swords as Saul led charge after charge against their ranks.

David followed Saul as best he could, his sword drawn, but he was constantly being jostled out of the way by Saul's veterans as they pressed forward to the Philistine line. The dust got in his throat and made him cough, in his eyes and made his vision blur. But he waded into the fray, his sword swinging, clipped a fellow Hebrew on the breastplate and nearly got himself killed.

David retired. He sat down on a rock, watching the deadly skirmish through the dust. Saul's helmet, a head above the others, marked the center of the fighting, his big sword flashing in the sunlight. Every so often, a Hebrew soldier would come staggering out of the melee, bleeding from an arm or head wound. David would run to him and try to help, wiping the blood off with the hem of his tunic. For the most part, the soldiers would simply grunt and charge back into the fighting. Two, however, lay down on the ground and slowly bled to death. David watched them, not knowing what to do. He tried to staunch one neck wound with his hand, but the blood simply pulsed through his fingers.

The Philistine circle finally broke, and David could see the feathered helmets moving fast down the Valley of Sorek with Saul's troops in pursuit. Hand-to-hand combatants would break out of the mass, stirring up the dust as metal clanged against metal to the final thrust or grapple. The trail of the retreating Philistines was littered with bodies—some Philistine, some Hebrew.

The fighting troops disappeared around a hill in the winding valley. David felt desperately bewildered and alone. He had failed Saul. He had failed himself. He had failed the Lord God. He would never make a soldier. He thought of running back to Gibeah in disgrace, losing himself among the women and children and never showing his face to Saul again. But as he wandered among the dead bodies in the empty valley, numb with his own defeat, he ached for Saul's strength, some gift of his manhood. But what could he do to deserve it?

Saul and his troops came marching up the valley again, talking, laughing, joking, easy in victory. David ran to meet Saul. "Let me carry your sword and shield."

"Ho-ho! Young David!" Saul's face was flushed, and his voice boomed. "I saw you fighting like a little lion! Just choose the right enemy next time!" His laughter was boisterous as he clapped him on the back.

David blushed crimson.

"But you *fight*, my boy. You'll make a great soldier some-day!" And he handed David his sword and shield. David clutched them as if they were his salvation, and fell into step a pace behind Saul.

Striding up the valley through the bodies, Saul stopped beside one Philistine lying on the ground, and poked at him with his foot. "David!"

David came forward.

"I think this is a prince or noble of Gath. Cut off his head, and we'll leave it on a spear."

David gulped. "Yes, my Lord."

Saul and his troops passed by, leaving David with two swords, a shield, and the Philistine lying motionless in the sun. Flies were buzzing around his lips and his closed eyes. His helmet lay on the ground nearby, and one side of his head was grotesquely swollen. The man was young, smooth-shaven, and he had a mole on his chin. His mouth was half-open, and David thought he saw the lips move slightly, but it was probably just the shimmer of the heat. The man looked dead.

David put Saul's sword and shield on the ground and took out his own sword. Saul would know—he'd tell him—that he had done it with his own sword. He stood back from the body on the ground, fighting a trembling in his gut, and raised the sword high above his head. With a mighty effort, he swung the sword downward. It bounced, and a gash showed in the man's shoulder, just above the armor.

The man's eyes opened.

The gash in the shoulder began to bleed.

The trembling shook David's whole body as he knelt down beside the man and tried to staunch the shoulder wound with his hand. He glanced at the man's eyes which seemed to be staring at the sky. Then they moved, and seemed to be staring at him. They were deep dark brown, and David felt that they looked at him from the distant mysteries of Sheol . . . inviting him . . . luring him seductively to the other side of life.

David pulled back, his eyes averted from the stare, and wrapped his arms around his knees to stop the shaking of his body. His teeth chattered. His mouth was dry. His own eyes glazed with tears.

Then, in memory, he heard the booming command of Saul's voice. He must bring the head to Saul. He could not fail the King.

His body still quaking, David grasped his sword and stood up. His knees were wobbly and he could not see very well, but he held the hilt of the sword tightly, its solidity his reassurance. He focused his blurred vision on the man's neck, just above the shoulder gash. He heard himself scream as he swung the sword down and felt it crunch against bone. Wiping his eyes, David saw that the man's mouth was now a gaping grimace, the cheeks torn, the jaw hanging open between face and neck.

David flung himself on the ground beside the man, hiding his own head in his arms, and felt spasm after spasm course through him as if lightning from the sky shot its bolts through him. He grasped the man's hand as it lay on the sand beside him. It was still warm. The man would take him to Sheol, usher him into the land of death. Holding the man's hand, he would walk through shrouding clouds into a place of peace.

His mind was lost in swirling vapors as he rose to his feet. His body moved as slowly as a dream as he picked up Saul's great sword. His muscles strained as he raised it above his head and let it come crashing down. For a moment, he stood there with his eyes shut. Then he opened them. The head lay a hand's span away from the body, gushing blood. All he could hear was the buzzing of flies around the pulp of the flesh.

David turned away and collapsed to the ground. Nausea surged inside him. He vomited, gasping after each acrid flood filled his mouth. Sweat poured out of his body and his head pulsed with pain.

He lay there on the sand, the stench of his own vomit sharp in his nostrils, until his body calmed. Then he staggered to his feet, every muscle aching, and picked up his own sword, wiped it with his tunic, and put it in his girdle. He picked up Saul's shield and slung it over his shoulder. He picked up Saul's sword and held it in his left hand. Finally, numbed, he leaned down and, with his right hand, grabbed the head by the hair and started walking up the valley of the Sorek to find Saul and his troops, the head dripping a trail of blood on the sand as he went.

Some of the troops were stretched out under the trees by the Sorek. Others were splashing around in the stream itself, shouting and laughing in its chill waters. Saul sat by the bank, his back against a tree trunk, talking with Abner and some of his other commanders, when David came up and bowed before the King.

"Our young warrior returns!" Saul said. "What took you so long?"

David laid the head down in front of Saul. "My aim. It's not as true as it should be."

Saul looked at the head. "I see." He glanced back at David, pride in his eyes. "But it was done. Your aim will get better."

"I hope so." And David laid Saul's sword and shield down beside him. Saul's sword had fresh bloodstains.

"Hah," said Saul. "You used my sword. I didn't think you could handle it." And there was just a glimmer of sharpness in his eyes.

David gave a feeble smile. "I thought there for a moment that no one but the King could handle it."

Saul's eyes grew warm again. "But you did. And that is good." He patted the ground. "Here, sit down beside me, my young warrior."

David sat down close to the King.

Saul looked out at the stream. "Jonathan!"

The figure of the prince emerged from the stream, dripping wet, wearing a loincloth, brushing the water from his eyes and hair. David watched his body as he came toward Saul. It was a godlike thing, all gleaming in the afternoon sunlight. He wondered if he would ever grow to be such a man.

But the prince paid no attention to David until Saul spoke. "Young David here has brought us a trophy."

Jonathan looked at the head, glanced at David, and said, "Oh."

"Get some of your men. Stick the head on a spear, and plant the spear in the ground. It will be a reminder to the people of Beth-shemesh of how the King defended them."

Jonathan nodded and picked up the head by the hair. "It can remind the Philistines as well." He walked away with the head, swinging it casually in his stride.

David moved. He did not know how he moved; his feet did not propel him. Still, he drifted in a fog so thick that all he could see before him was the back of another figure drifting as he was through the opaqueness. He must follow the figure. He knew that. Yet he could not will the drift. It might sweep him away until he was lost in some desperate solitude. All he could do was concentrate on the figure in front of him, and hope by some force to keep it near him.

The swirl of the fog quickened, and David felt an icy chill that seemed to come from caverns or a great gray sea. He was suspended in the drift, helpless against the chill that could sap his body of life. All he could hope for was the warmth of the figure ahead of him. But the distance between them seemed immense.

David gathered all his will to pull himself to the figure

through the void, urging himself moment by moment, hand's breadth by hand's breadth toward the imagined warmth. He would feel himself move forward in an eddy of the fog, and then the figure would move another arm's length farther away. The chill would sink deeper into David's being, and his fear would grow.

Finally a gust of dank and foggy air lifted him and carried him so close he could reach out and touch the figure's shoulder. His whole spirit leapt at the contact, grasping the solidity of flesh, the surety of another being.

And then the figure turned and David saw its face—the deep dark eyes, the gaping cheeks, the sundered jaw. . . .

He was suddenly awake, shaking in the darkness, not knowing where he was, only that the fog and the figure had vanished.

Then he heard Saul groan, and his great body heave and turn in sleep. David almost cried with relief; he could find warmth.

He slipped off his pallet, felt the night air cool on his naked body. He pulled back Saul's coverlet and lay down beside him, tugging the coverlet back over them. Turning on his side, he pressed himself against the warmth of Saul's big back, and eased one arm around to his chest, his fingers feeling a bristle of hair.

Saul's hand, in a slow, sleep-drenched movement, took David's hand on his chest, and pulled it closer till David could feel the faint steady thump of his heart.

Feeling warm and protected, David went to sleep.

When he awoke the next morning, he was lying on his back. Saul was still asleep, with one arm across David's chest. David moved off the pallet with stealth, stood up, and put on his tunic. He was sure—at least he hoped—that Saul did not know that he had spent the night in Saul's arms. But he also knew that he would like to spend another night there.

However, fearing Saul's anger, David spent the next two

nights chaste on his own pallet, nestled under his coverlet against the chill night air, and hoping that no dreams would cause him to panic.

The next evening, with the troops encamped in the nearby Valley of Elah, David found his brother Shammah, who had just returned from a patrol with a report for the King. He saw the glint of pride in Shammah's eye as David stood close by the King, Saul's great shield slung over his shoulder. As a gesture to the house of Jesse, Saul excused David to spend some evening hours with Shammah before returning for the night, and David tagged along with Shammah, going to his camp upstream.

One of Shammah's knees was bandaged in linen and he limped slightly. David, with visions of fierce battle going around in his head, asked him what had happened. Shammah shrugged a bit sheepishly. "I got caught in a bramble. I think it was a Philistine bramble. On night patrol, watch out for brambles."

David nodded. "I've never gone on a night patrol."

"Don't hurry," said Shammah. "You've got enough to learn."

"I know."

The two brothers sat down beside the stream of Elah. Shammah unstrapped his armor and let it rest on the ground beside him, rubbing his shoulders after he had done so. "The left side chafes," he complained. "I think the leather's worn."

David examined the shoulder strap. "The leather's all right. But here . . . one plate's bent in."

Shammah peered over David's shoulder. "You're right. Too bad I don't have an armor-bearer like the King."

"I'll fix it." He put the plate between two stones and hammered with one of them until the plate straightened. He examined the armor again, and looked at Shammah reproachfully. "It needs polishing."

Shammah grinned. "I'm a mere soldier, my Lord."

"Don't 'my Lord' me."

"Why not? You're as close to the King as Abner." He shook his head. "Our father was amazed when we told him."

"I serve Saul, that's all. Anyone could do for him what I do."

"The difference is . . ." and Shammah poked a finger on David's chest, ". . . the King wants *you* to do it. The house of Jesse is blessed as none of the rest of us could make it blessed."

"But you have fought for him . . . for Israel. All I could do was play the harp."

"Enough, David. Apparently enough." He patted David on the shoulder. "We are proud of you."

David felt a certain disturbing awe, the feeling he had had when Samuel had pressed his oily thumb against David's forehead. The skies seemed to press in on him, and he wanted to hide to avoid the weight. What was expected of him? And . . . would he fail, and what would be the cost of that failure? Here he was faced with no mere flock of sheep, but kingdoms of men.

It was dark when David returned to the royal tent after his hours with Shammah. The flaps were closed and David thought Saul had already gone to sleep. But entering the tent, he found a lamp lit and Saul lying naked on his pallet, a goblet of wine by his side. The body seemed more massive in the closeness of the tent as the flickering lights and shadows played across it. He knew the feel of it—the gnarl of the bones' joints, the hardness of the muscle, the matting of hair. But its sheer presence, laid out before him, was fearsome and pulse-quickening.

Saul looked at him with steady, heavy-lidded eyes, but he said nothing. David felt impaled by the stare. He shifted uneasily. "May I cover you, my Lord?"

"No." And Saul took a draft from his wine goblet.

"Shall I wash your feet?"

"No. I have washed them already."

"Shall I fill your wine goblet?"

"No. It is full enough."

David did not know what else to say. In the silence, he looked at Saul's steady eyes and then, flustered, turned his gaze to the lamp.

Saul's voice was low, but commanding. "Take off your tunic."

David did as he was told.

"Now, take off your loincloth and sandals."

David slipped out of his loincloth and undid his sandals with trembling hands. He stood naked before the King.

A silence.

Saul's voice was soft. "You are well formed, boy."

"Thank you, my Lord."

"Turn around, slowly, that I may see all of you." His words were slightly slurred, and David felt a flash of fear as he turned his back on the King. What was all that wine doing to the King's head? He suddenly thought of swinging around and throwing himself into the King's arms to staunch whatever spirits might possess him. But he stood there, facing the tent wall, sensing the King's gaze coursing down his back. The muscles of his buttocks tightened.

He turned back to face Saul, aching to be held in those arms, aching to rest beside that big body. But the presence he saw was foreboding. He felt tethered by those heavy-lidded eyes, captive of the strength so casually strewn on the pallet. He wanted to run from the tent, but he dared not move. He was at the King's command.

And the King commanded. "Come here, boy."

David stepped toward the pallet. Saul reached up, grasped his wrist, and with a wrench pulled him down till he lay flat on his back beside the King. Rising on one elbow, Saul drank again from the wine goblet, and wiped his mouth with his hand. "So . . . now you're where you want to be, eh?"

"As you wish, my Lord."

"Ha! As *you* wish, boy. I know how you tucked your pretty rump against me."

"I had dreams. Bad dreams. I needed someone . . ."

"Well, I'll give you something to dream about."

Saul's presence loomed as he laid his heavy hands on David's shoulders and twisted to turn him over. David saw the King's penis swell, dark and lethal in a forest of hair. The hands on his shoulders pressed harder. David stiffened his body. "Saul! No!"

"What do you mean, 'no'?" Saul's eyes blazed.

"Not like this!"

"Like what I say! Roll over, boy, and spread that pretty rump."

David was rigid. "No!"

David felt the crash of the blow on his cheek. He twisted out of Saul's grasp and lurched to his feet, panting and trembling. Saul made a lunge for him, but he dodged, and Saul fell back on the pallet with a grunt, rubbing his hand slowly across his forehead.

The words came out of David like sobs. "I serve you, Saul. You are a giant to me. I give you my faith. I would give you my body. I would follow you to Sheol. But I am not slut flesh."

"So . . . I see courage." Saul's voice was slurred and weary. "You will make a great warrior someday, boy."

"Boy? Boy! If that is all you want, get yourself another boy. I am David, son of Jesse. I am David of Bethlehem. And I came to serve a mighty King . . ." his voice broke, ". . . with all my heart!"

David turned away, and put on his tunic and sandals. He did not see two great tears fill Saul's eyes as he fled the tent.

David walked through the night, higher and higher into the hills on his way to Bethlehem. He wondered at what

101

he had done. He feared Saul's rage and those blazing eyes. How had he summoned the courage to confront them? How had he pitted "David of Bethlehem" against the King? Still, barely thinking, he had. And yet, once he returned to his father's house, he knew he'd be back with the sheep while Shammah and his other brothers would reap glory in Saul's army. "David of Bethlehem" would be roaming the Judean hills like any other shepherd. No special light would fall on him. The eyes of Samuel would not search him out again.

At the crest of a hill, he lingered. Ahead were the high hills and Bethlehem; behind him, the Valley of Elah and Saul's encampment. The moonlight glossed the pitch and roll of the landscape. He could find his way in either direction. He could turn back. Saul would be in wine-drenched sleep and probably wake up the next morning with no memory of the night before, and David could pretend that nothing had happened. Life would go on.

Until the next drunken evening when Saul sought slut-flesh and pinioned David to be temple dog to the King's whim? He might not be able to get away the next time. And "David of Bethlehem" would no longer be the anointed of Samuel, but only a body for the King to penetrate at his pleasure.

Still, looking back toward Elah, David ached. There was grandeur to Saul, grandeur that he had seen in no other man. He wanted to draw upon Saul, capture his essence and make it his own. He would grasp a storm, hold a flood of waters in his arms, carry a mountain on his shoulders, and know the mysteries of the Great Sea. All the elements were bound in Saul, and his wonder at the man was a kind of love, as deep as any he had felt.

But who was he to cope with such a love? How could he draw Saul to himself if he were only baggage in the encampment? He had a wonder, too, to offer Saul. He did not know its nature—only that Samuel had seen it and marked it on his forehead. Somehow that mark was sacred; it had made him "David of Bethlehem." He would give his body to Saul —gladly—but there on the hill's crest he knew that, whatever else might happen, he would not be plundered of that special self. It was his gift to Saul, and if Saul could not accept it with grace, Saul would not have it.

David walked on toward Bethlehem.

He arrived at Jesse's house at dawn to find his father at his morning meal of bread, figs, and honey. Jesse embraced him and offered him food. But as David ate, Jesse kept looking at him quizzically, his gnarled farmer's hands toying with a fig. "You seem troubled, David."

David kept his eyes on the bread in front of him. "It is strange at the King's court."

"A change from here, I'm sure. But it is a great honor for this house that you are there."

"I know. Shammah told me."

"Yes. You are armor-bearer to the King himself. A great honor."

David looked his father straight in the eye and realized, not having seen him for several months, that Jesse was getting old. His beard was almost white in places and his eyes were watery. The lines on his face were the work of many seasons. David sensed, to his misery, that he was his father's final gift of pride from a lifetime of patient effort. It was as if the King himself now honored this sturdy farmer. And how would that sturdy farmer know that the King was intent on plundering his son? What was David to say? "Father, our great King tried to rape me last night?" David recoiled. Jesse had such faith in his God and his King. David felt entrusted with the old man's heart.

David spoke gently. "Father, I would like to stay here and go back to tending the flocks."

"You? Here? But . . . the King . . . ?"

"I do not believe I can serve the King in the ways he wants to be served."

Jesse frowned. "But, surely . . ."

David cut in. "I am worthy on the harp. But I do not know the ways of battle."

"You are young. You can learn. It comes easily to Shammah and the others."

David shook his head, his eyes now averted again. "Perhaps someday. Not now."

Jesse put his hand on David's. "You have been traveling all night?"

David nodded.

"Then you should sleep. Things may look different when you wake."

David lay on his pallet in his old room and watched the sunlight come through the window lattice, making patterns on the mud-brick of the opposite wall. Outside, he could hear the bleating of sheep and the talk of women going to the well. His eyes traced the familiar cracks in the roof-beams as he nestled under the coverlet and felt the ache beginning to drain from his muscles. What had it been, that time in Gibeah? A dream?

When he woke, it was darkening. He could hear men's voices, talking earnestly. One of the voices was Jesse's. The other sounded like Shammah, but what was Shammah doing at Bethlehem?

David slipped on his tunic and sandals, and went into the big room. Shammah was there, sitting across the table from Jesse, drinking a cup of wine. He looked worried—very worried. And David felt suddenly very guilty. But he tried to sound innocent. "You've come home, too, Shammah?"

"I have come home to get you," said Shammah firmly, "and return you to Saul."

"It appears the King has missed you," Jesse added.

"Missed me?"

"He grieves for you," said Shammah. "And when the King grieves in one room, he rages in another."

104

Both men's eyes were on him, and David felt himself pinioned and squirming. He gestured awkwardly. "The King has better servants than me." But even as he spoke, Shammah's words were searing to David. "He grieves for you." As David grieved for Saul, but could not say so. Was it . . . that Saul . . . knew? Had their thoughts mingled over miles that night? Would he take David's gift as Saul had gifted David with his favor? He would go back, he would run, he would kneel in homage if that were so!

David looked at Shammah sharply. "Did you see Saul?"

"Yes. This morning. He called me to him at his tent. He was red-eyed with drink from the night before and his talk was heavy."

"What did he say?" David tried to hide the waver in his voice, tried to keep back the tears in his eyes.

"He asked me where you were. I said I did not know. He said he knew. I asked him how it was. He said nothing for a moment, and when he spoke, his voice was hoarse, like a man greatly burdened. He said to me, 'He is David of Bethlehem. Go to Bethlehem and find him and bring him to me. For David is favored of the King.' "

No one in the room spoke.

David stood with his fists clenched, trying to control the storming exaltation within him. He felt as he had felt when his father and brothers had looked at him after Samuel had anointed him. A wonder. A pride. And a fear.

He spoke slowly. "I will go . . . with you . . . to Saul."

Saul was sitting beside a campfire with Jonathan, Abner, and several others of the court when David returned the following evening. David approached the King. No one paid him any particular notice except Saul, who gave him one long look, and then turned back to Abner.

David noticed the shield beside Saul. He reached down, picked it up, and slung it over his shoulder. "Needs polishing," he murmured to Saul, who nodded, just the hint of a smile on his face. But David caught it and gave just a wisp of an answering smile. Saul returned to affairs of state while David trudged back to the royal tent with the shield. He got a bowl of water, a linen cloth, and some fine sand, and sat down inside the tent to burnish the bronze. It gave him something to do with his hands, and right then, he needed something to do with his hands. Otherwise, they shook.

He did not know what he would say to the King, once they were alone, or what the King would say to him. He almost hoped Saul would be so sotted with wine when he came to the tent that no one would have to say anything. But he quickly hoped that Saul would be sober. Meanwhile he kept polishing the shield, admiring its glint in the lamplight.

Saul entered the tent, his big frame towering in the closeness, his eyes brooding as they looked at David. The youth sprang to his feet. "May I help you unlatch your armor, my Lord?"

"Yes. That would be good." He turned his back to David, who undid the straps, eased the armor off his shoulders, and set it upon the ground.

Saul rubbed his shoulders, and turned to face David. He reached out a hand and tousled David's hair. "I missed you, David of Bethlehem."

"I am here, my Lord." The smile on his face was bashful. "I did not stay away very long." With a sudden impulse, he put his arms around Saul's waist, and rested his head on his chest. He felt Saul's arms close around him.

They stood that way for a long moment in silence, David listening to the sonorous beat of Saul's heart.

Finally David pulled back and stood straight, his head slightly bowed, the model figure of a proper servant. "Shall I wash your feet, my Lord?"

Saul shook his head. "I washed them in the stream—before I knew you had returned."

David looked abashed.

"But you . . . you have traveled long," Saul said. "Lie down. Your aches may need a healing."

106

David looked into Saul's eyes, his own heartbeat pounding. Then he took off his tunic and lay, face down, on Saul's pallet. He rested his head on his arm and closed his eyes.

He sensed Saul beside him. Then he felt the chill of oil being poured just below his shoulders, and smelled a fragrance. Saul's warm hand moved where the oil had been poured, rubbing gently from one shoulder to the other. David felt his tensions begin to ebb, and as the rubbing continued with a steady pressure further down his spine, a lassitude seemed to envelop him. He felt as yielding as the sand.

"Saul," he whispered.

"Yes?"

"Be with me. Inside me."

David gasped with pain as he felt himself entered. But the pain was quickly gone as he was filled with flesh, and the lassitude flowed back over him. Then, in throb after throb, he received Saul's essence.

When the moment passed, David eased himself to his side. His head rested on one of Saul's arms. He pulled the other arm over across his chest. He tightened his muscles to keep Saul within him. So David rested.

SIX

T he waters of the Jordan shimmered gold and gray in the
evening light. The sun still cast its colors on the bluffs
of Gilead, but the cliffs below were in ominous shadow.

Joab was insistent. "We must ford this evening. On the
other side, we are reasonably safe. Absalom would not risk
a ford in darkness."

David, sitting on a rock with his bare feet resting in a riverside pool, nodded. "We are blessed. The water is low."

"There are still deep spots to watch for."

"I know. I fell in one once. I thought it would take me to
Sheol."

"Abishai will lead the mule drivers and the mules. I will
lead you and your court next, while the mercenaries hold the
west bank. Then Benaiah will lead the troops across."

David knew Joab's plan was sound and cautious, assuming
the worst might happen with Absalom's troops pressing close
behind. But still he was puzzled. No dust rose on the road up
into the hills to Jerusalem. The rear guard had reported no
pursuing detachments. Absalom, it seemed, was simply letting his disheveled father slip away like a whipped dog.

David stared at the bluffs of Gilead. He knew he could regroup there. Did Absalom have so little respect that he

thought the dog might not recover? Or was he, out of some last remains of filial piety, leaving his father to live out his last days in impoverished exile in Gilead? David snorted. He hoped Absalom knew his father better than that! Watching the mule caravan cross the Jordan, David felt a rekindling of hope. Absalom had let opportunity fall at his feet. Such opportunity, David hoped, would not come to Absalom again.

Still . . . David's thought turned back on itself . . . he had hoped before. Now, in middle age, he could look back at all the hopes he had vested in others, and how, one by one, those hopes had gone ashen. Saul dead. Jonathan dead. Ishbosheth dead. Michal despising him. The Temple still only a vision. And now even his own son . . . With Absalom turned against him, even his belief in himself was shaken. Perhaps Absalom was right. The whipped dog might stay cowed in Gilead, or held tethered by the Ammonites in Rabbah. So would end the life of the once-great king who had built an empire for Israel.

David watched his son Solomon playing gleefully in the riverside pool where David was soaking his feet. The water glistening in his hair, Solomon scooped his hand and with a peal of laughter tossed a sprinkling of water at David. David feigned royal anger, and then, reaching down till his back twinged, scooped a spray of water back to Solomon. His son, shrieking like a drowning man, ran through the water to David and flung himself in his lap, his laughter now coming in gasps.

"Let's stay here, Father. I *like* it. And we can play!"

David gathered him up into his lap, while Bathsheba dried his hair with her shawl.

"Can we? Can we? I want to stay here!"

"No, Solomon, we are going to cross the river to the high country."

Solomon was doubtful. "What's over there?"

"Oh . . . sun and sand, wind and stars . . ."

"That's not much."

". . . and friends of your father's."

109

"And boys to play with?"

"Of course." David hesitated. "And flocks of sheep."

"Ugh!"

"Don't turn your nose in the air, young prince. You may be tending them just like your father did."

Solomon straightened and held out his arms as if to embrace all the western hills. "I am to rule over all of Israel and Judah. That's what Mother told me."

David glanced at Bathsheba, sitting beside him, but she averted her eyes.

"Oh," said David, and he sighed. "Well, Solomon, let me tell you about tending sheep."

Solomon sighed right back. "You've *told* me about tending sheep! I don't want to hear any more about sheep. They smell."

"They give the wool for your clothes . . . the meat that you eat . . ."

"And they smell," said Solomon, disposing of the subject.

David felt abashed. He turned to Bathsheba. "I think Prince Solomon is getting a little too princely."

Bathsheba smiled. But David was grim. "Have I failed again?"

Before Bathsheba could answer, Solomon wrapped his arms around David's neck. "Father, carry me across the river."

Bathsheba murmured, "Your back, David."

"If my son wants me to carry him across the river," David said, "I'll carry him across the river."

The last of the mule train had stepped into the water when Joab came bustling up to David. "All right, my Lord, we go."

David rose from the rock and straightened himself.

Joab pointed upstream. "The shallowest place is about twenty paces up there."

Joab led the way. David followed, holding Bathsheba by one hand and Solomon by the other.

As they came to the fording place, a gang of Canaanite boys came running downstream in the shallow water that

110

they made splash over their naked bodies. They were laughing and shouting. As they came close, David could make out what they were saying. It was a kind of cheer. "Hebrew! Hebrew! Go back where you came from! Hebrew! Hebrew! Get out of Canaan!"

A couple of the mercenaries started to give chase to the boys, who dodged out of their way, laughing and splashing. David sent Ira to call the mercenaries back. "We've killed enough Canaanites," said David.

The members of the court glowered at the Canaanites as the boys stood out of reach, chanting, and wiggling their long foreskins at the circumcised.

David turned to Joab. "Put Solomon on my shoulders."

"David, you can barely walk yourself!"

"It is a short way. I will carry him across."

Joab was exasperated. "David . . . !"

"Put . . . the child . . . on my shoulders."

Joab did as he was told, muttering. Solomon clamped his legs around David's neck, took a firm hold on one of David's ears, and let out a whoop.

David stepped into the waters of the Jordan. He walked slowly, letting his feet get a good grip on the sandy bottom as the water flowed around his knees. Joab held one arm, still muttering under his breath, while Bathsheba had an arm around his waist. Behind them came a long line of people of the court.

David, the King, was passing out of Israel. Was this the harbinger of what the Canaanite boys had chanted? Would Absalom be next? Would he bring the Ark to solace the tribes of Jacob in more years of wandering and promises from the Lord? Jerusalem. It had been such a hope! The golden city between the lands of Israel and Judah, the Temple, resting place of the Ark and of all the tribes, the heart of the promise fulfilled. It was David's city. It was his offering to the Lord.

Still, like everything else in Canaan, it had had to be seized. Joab and his men had done it, climbing up the water shaft from Kidron right into the citadel and taking the

Jebusites, who had built the fortress, by surprise. After a night of slaughter, Joab and his men had opened the north gate and let David and his troops into the city. David had walked in triumph down a street of death to give thanks to the Lord.

Now he wondered at that triumph. What he had seized, the Jebusites could take back. Would they take courage at the news that their conqueror had fled, and mobilize their forces? Would Absalom and his patchwork troops be able to hold them off? Or would Jerusalem be lost?

The thought was gall to David. In the middle of the Jordan he almost stopped, almost shouted an order to turn back to save the Holy City. But Joab and Bathsheba guided him firmly on to the Gilead shore. David knew that there were some things that Joab would not tolerate, and hysterical military decisions were among them.

The flow was faster in the middle of the river and the water deeper, now lapping against David's thighs. Solomon's wiry young body was growing heavy on his shoulders, and the grip Solomon now had on David's hair hurt his scalp. But the opposite shore was getting near and David was determined to push on, disregarding the beat of pain in his back. The river bottom under his feet was pebbly and he stepped cautiously to avoid stones.

But he stepped on a flat rock that tilted under his weight. David's foot twisted and he lurched forward. The last he heard before the water engulfed him was Solomon's whoop as he fell off his shoulders. Joab dragged him to his feet, dripping, coughing, and sputtering. But once David had brushed the water from his eyes, he saw Solomon just a few paces ahead of him, standing in water barely up to his knees. "You were playing!" he yelled. "Father was playing!"

As David floundered around, Solomon held out his arm. "Come on, Father, take my hand."

David climbed to the sandy shoal where Solomon stood. Hand in hand, Solomon led David to the Gilead shore.

*　*　*

112

The night was dark. A new moon shone in the western sky, casting a gossamer reflection on the waters of the Jordan. David, sitting on the Gilead shore with Ira, could see the ripples in the center of the river, but the pools protected by the shoals near the shore seemed still as silver. Across the river, soldiers of the rearguard encampment moved like ghosts, barely visible, but all he could hear were murmuring voices, the occasional snort of a mule, or the clank of metal against metal. No campfires burned anywhere except far up in the western hills where shepherds tended their flocks. David was king of the specters. But for his back, he would have thought himself disembodied.

"Would you not sleep, my Lord?" Ira asked.

"I would. Indeed, I would. But I have to wait."

"Oh?"

"Joab and his men are hunting some cave . . . or pit . . . or thicket. Someplace to hide the sacred carcass of the King. Oh, yes, Ira, it is all right for a mere mortal like you to sleep out here under the stars, or snuggle down in a tent. But the King? The King's safety must be preserved. And what does that mean? I'll tell you. Once I was being hidden from the Ammonites up here in one of these bluffs. They found me a cave. Not a large cave, but pleasant enough with a nice view of the river. So I settled down for the night, a guard posted at the mouth of the cave. I felt envious of the troops stretched out in their tents on the sand. The floor of the cave was stone, and as I tried to go to sleep, the stench in the place got worse and worse. But it had been a hard day, and I went to sleep anyway.

"Then, in the middle of the night, I heard this terrible commotion, and the guard was yelling at me to wake up. I reared up off my pallet and came to the mouth of the cave, where the guard and I confronted a bear. A large and angry bear. A bear who wanted his cave back.

"Now, you know, Ira, I could have really given the scribes something to write about if I had killed that bear. Who knows? They may write about it anyway and make

113

me into another Samson. But the truth is, the guard and I ran for our lives. And I finished the night out under the stars, where I had wanted to be in the first place.

"But I got thinking, before I went to sleep. Here I was, weary of the Lord's Will that I should kill Canaanites, Philistines, Ammonites, and Amalekites. Was it also the Lord's Will that I should kill bears? Especially a bear who only wanted his cave back?"

"As you say, my Lord, you grow weary. The Lord's Will sometimes strains us all."

The very smoothness of Ira's voice annoyed David. "Weary? Is that all? Just weary?"

"I warrant that ten years ago, you'd have had Shimei cut to pieces, and those Canaanite boys drowned in the Jordan. But you let Shimei throw stones at you and the Canaanite boys taunt you."

"Yes. And I do not regret it."

"But the Lord is a fierce God."

"And He demands that I be ready to sacrifice Absalom as Abraham was called upon to sacrifice Isaac? Is that it?"

"If it is for the good of Israel."

Tears welled up in David's eyes. "I will . . . not . . . go . . . to Moriah."

Ira was silent.

"No," said David. "No. No. No. If I am weary, so be it. If my faith is thin, I confess it. If I am less than Abraham or Saul, I will know it. But I will not bind Absalom to the altar!"

"But Saul, so it is said, was determined to kill you. And you were his son-in-law. He was as fierce, they say, as Samuel when he slew Agag in the Lord's name."

David gave Ira a long, baleful look. "Do you think Saul tried to kill me in the Lord's name?"

"It is said you threatened the Lord's anointed and the rightful King."

David erupted. " 'It is said.' 'It is said.' 'It is said.' Ha! And now that I have been king, it *will* be said that I was

114

the Lord's anointed by Samuel, and Saul was the wrongful king and visited with an Evil Spirit! Oh, yes, what is said . . . it depends . . . it changes . . . What was said when I was in exile and serving the Philistines is very different from what is said of me now! Yet *then* it was 'the Lord's Will.' And *now* it is 'the Lord's Will.' But only as it is *said* to be 'the Lord's Will.' And who knows what will be said if Absalom holds Jerusalem?"

Ira shifted uneasily. "My Lord, you twist words. It is our faith that the Lord works His Will through us."

"Whichever way the battle goes, eh? Well, let me tell you, Ira, under the arch of heaven. No Evil Spirit visited Saul. I drew Saul's anger to myself. Through my ambition. Through my pride. And through my will. His anger, visited on me, was foreseen and deserved. If the Lord's Will moved among us, it moved in mysterious ways. And it cannot be easily said."

David had become Saul's armor-bearer when he was fifteen years old and continued to serve him as years passed. His height increased, although he never grew as tall as Saul. His body became more rugged. The hair on his face became a short beard. He tried to imitate Saul's stride, but his legs weren't long enough. He tried to mimic Saul's voice, and lowered his own impressively, but he could never achieve Saul's boom of command. Still, in the shadow of Saul, he had stature. He could feel pride when commanders gave messages to him to relay to Saul. He liked the deference shown him as companion to the King. He especially reveled in the way Shammah and his other brothers sought his counsel as a reflection of the mind of Saul. Often he gave them some of his own mind, too.

But David's life with Saul was the life of the field. Back at Gibeah, Saul lived in a house he had had since before he was anointed King of Israel and Judah, with his wife Ahinoam and several of his younger sons and daughters. David shared a tent with Saul's son Ishbosheth, while the older sons, such as Jonathan, had tents of their own. David saw Saul only at evening meal in the royal tent, and though he sat close to the throne and frequently played the harp after the evening meal was finished, his distance from Saul was a formal distance, broken only by an occasional exchange of glances or a few spoken words. David would wait anxiously for Saul to announce another foray in the field where David could feel himself restored to the King's intimacy.

He began to notice Jonathan more frequently, at evening meal or hunched in counsel with Saul in the field. He watched how Jonathan moved, how he carried his head. He admired the strength of his hands, more sinuous than Saul's, and the decisive way he moved them. He envied the assurance of Jonathan's command. Saul wore his power as naturally as his skin. But Jonathan wore it with pride like a multicolored cloak, giving it an occasional flourish that seemed to dazzle those who took his orders.

But while David kept watching Jonathan, Jonathan paid little heed to David. He seemed to regard David as just another servant or slave—necessary baggage in the business of living. His words were brisk. His attention focused elsewhere. Nor was he impressed in the slightest with David's closeness to Saul. He had his own ties with Saul, and no need of David. In fact, the times when Jonathan was with Saul were the only times when David felt ignored by Saul, and he simmered in a double jealousy, sitting on the sidelines, staring at those two magnificent men. They seemed so close, and yet he noticed how Jonathan gave his father a kind of loyal deference that did not seem called upon for Saul-as-father or Saul-as-King. Jonathan gave his loyalty to the man. David felt a further jealousy. He could never give such loyalty to his own father, Jesse.

Only occasionally in the field did David have any contact with Jonathan alone. And once, when he did, the incident was disturbing to David.

David was sitting outside the royal tent one evening in

the field, polishing some leather thongs, when Jonathan came up—he looked like a giant from where David sat—and demanded to know where Saul was. David said he did not know, but, with a shy smile, said he thought Saul would be back soon, and would my Lord wait? Jonathan nodded, a gruff expression on his face, and sat down beside David.

A skirmish with the Philistines had gone well for the Israelites that day, and David was enthusiastic. "They fled as if they were scourged by the Lord!"

Jonathan tossed a pebble into the air. "To fight another day."

"Not soon, with the whipping we gave them!"

"A night's rest, and they'll try an ambush. They are good fighters and they have the iron."

"But we have the Lord."

Jonathan looked at David. "Yes, when He is not angered."

"But . . . but . . ."

"Your faith is young, David."

"And yours?"

Jonathan shrugged. "They've defeated us before. They'll defeat us again. My father and I . . . we'll meet them again in Sheol."

David felt panic. "It cannot happen. No! It cannot happen! Not to Saul." He hesitated. "Not to you."

Jonathan grinned at David's evident alarm. "Be at peace, young one. We're not planning on it."

The first break had come when David had been Saul's armor-bearer for three years. He was now eighteen, sturdy and a little more than medium height. Carrying Saul's sword, shield, and helmet was not the chore it had been, and Saul put more responsibility on him for tasks not usually done by armor-bearers. Sometimes he served as courier, other times as surrogate, and he fought shoulder-to-shoulder with the King in battle. He no longer lingered on the outer fringes of tactical and strategic councils, but sat close behind the King, listening and sometimes whispering a forgotten detail in Saul's ear. Saul came to rely on him as an extension of himself, but David was careful to be self-effacing in front of Abner, Jonathan, and Saul's other commanders. He only lorded it over his brother, Shammah. Shammah wouldn't tell.

But at night, in the privacy of the field tent, David was as naked as ever to Saul's needs and pleasures. Yet they were his needs and pleasures, too. As the vocabulary of their bodies grew, David learned to express a variety of relationships beyond his imaginings. Sometimes, to his wonderment, he would assault a pliant king. At other times, dressing a battle wound somewhere on Saul's great body, he would feel a flow of encompassing tenderness. He would sit, mothering Saul's head in his lap, as the big man groaned with pain or cursed the Philistine who'd got him. David felt as if he held a child.

Following the King on his marches, or on his rounds at encampments, David tried to be as inconspicuous as any loyal servant. But, knowing his true place, he kept a possessive eye on Saul. He was the keeper of the King's body. He was the keeper of those ranges of his spirit that were hidden from any other warrior who marched with him. He guarded Saul's soul.

David would remember those several years of closeness with Saul as some of the happiest of his life. He would later be wrenched by the tug and pull of many responsibilities, all vying for his attention and decision. But then he had only one responsibility, and he could give himself to it without stint, knowing that what he freely gave was deeply needed. He could feel the grip of Saul's hand on his shoulder, see the look in his eyes, cradle the body and feel the muscles drain of tension. He sensed the urgency of Saul's reaching hand in sleep. For this great King, David knew pity. And he also knew his own worth.

As a great king himself, David would never be quite sure of it again.

118

* * *

One evening in Gibeah, David sat outside his tent, practicing his harp. Saul was in his house with his wife and
children. David's tent-mate, Ishbosheth, was not in a
friendly mood. The Israelite troops had not been in the field
for over a month. He felt all his energies languish in the
heat of the night. David, at eighteen, was bored. No sweet
music from his harp could assuage his lassitude. No triviali-
ties of the court could staunch his sense of waste. He yearned
for the body of Saul, the noise of battle, and Philistine blood.

He put his harp back inside the tent and went down the
path to find his brother Shammah. Shammah was drowsing
inside his tent. David gave him an imperious poke in the
ribs. "Come. It's too hot to sleep. Let's take a walk."

Shammah gave a groan of protest. But David was the
King's armor-bearer. Shammah got up.

High on a knoll on the outskirts of Gibeah, David and
Shammah sat and enjoyed the coolness of the breeze off the
Great Sea. But the coolness seemed only to sharpen David's
disquietness, and being with Shammah stirred his remem-
brance of Bethlehem and his anointment by Samuel. It
seemed as if he could almost smell the smoke of the burning
carcass, know the force of those burning eyes.

"Shammah . . ."

"Yes?"

"Why aren't we in the field?"

"I don't know." He shrugged. "It's good to have a rest."

"I've had a rest."

"Why are you asking me, anyway? You know Saul's mind
better than any of us."

"When we march, I know. But now it's all talk, talk, talk
with the tribal elders in the royal tent. And what's to be
done by talk, talk, talk?"

"Sometimes it saves a battle," said Shammah. "Or makes
a victory out of defeat."

"Talk's boring." David got to his feet and put a pebble in

119

his sling. He pointed out into the darkness. "See? I'll hit that rock over there."

"I'll bet you can't."

"I can!" David whirled his sling and let the pebble fly. There was a sharp clink of stone on stone.

"You missed," said Shammah.

"No, I didn't!"

"Yes, you did. It hit another rock."

"It didn't!" David pushed Shammah down on the ground and sat on him. "I hit the rock I said I was going to hit. I did!"

Shammah struggled to sit up again, but David held him. "Ha-ha. You're getting strong, aren't you, young one?"

"Strong enough to hold you or any Philistine!"

"So you think!" said Shammah, and with a mighty twist pushed David off.

David sprawled on the ground, laughing. But suddenly he grew very solemn. "Shammah . . ."

"Yes?"

"I want a command."

"You're too young, yet."

"I'm fully grown. I fight beside the King. I sit with him in councils. I know as much as some of his commanders. Saul's taught me."

"How to make men follow you?"

David's voice was loud and sharp. "I can command. In the name of Saul, I can command."

He saw Shammah looking at him, a long look, as if he had never seen him before.

"Just a hundred men," David went on. "Just a hundred for sudden raids and skirmishes. I could be out there, bringing victory for the Lord . . . while Saul sits with the elders and talks and talks and talks . . ."

Shammah's voice was deliberate. "If Saul gave you a command you would not be with him. You would be off someplace in the field. Just another commander. But as it is now, you are always with him in the field. You bring honor to the house of Jesse. You help us all."

"I would not leave Saul! No, I would be with him. It's just that . . . I would be a commander. Let some youth carry his armor. No boy could stand between me and Saul. I will be with him always! But don't you see? It's just . . . just . . . just that I have grown."

"Do you think that Saul will grant you a command?"

David spoke softly in the darkness. "I have ways with Saul."

David's command was a handpicked force, none much older than himself, and they endured, with silent stoicism, muttered references to the "baby brigade." His lieutenants were two young demons named Joab and Abishai who, in the judgment of some of the older commanders, were bent on suicide. But Saul, once the force was formed, looked upon it with unabashed pride and would regale his other commanders, much to their disgust, with the exploits of the juveniles. Jonathan was especially repelled and saw the whole matter as a sign of Saul's premature dotage.

But David could not have cared less what anyone but Saul thought. The force to him was Saul's right arm, just as he himself was a part of Saul, grown now to serve the King a hundredfold. Only one thing bothered David—the scrawny, pimply-faced young Danite named Arad that Saul had taken as his new armor-bearer. David could not stand Arad, and he fretted that Arad would not wash the King's feet, would not polish his shield, could not cope with him when he was heavy with wine. He dared not think of them in bed together; the thought was too repulsive. Out on training marches, David would make sure his force returned to the main camp by nightfall, just to make sure that such a terrible thing never happened. Arad would sleep outside the tent-flap. David slept with Saul. The arrange-

121

ment was so customary that no one bothered to comment—except Arad, who grumbled, particularly when it rained. But who cared about some scrawny, pimply-faced Danite child who couldn't polish a shield right?

As nearly as anyone among the Israelites could figure out, the Philistine god Dagon had for some reason become enraged, and the Philistines were on a rampage, evidently determined to kill every son of Jacob they could find. Leaving their precious chariots behind, columns from the five cities moved up into the hill country, looting, pillaging, burning crops, and herding livestock back to the plains. They attacked Beth-shemesh, feinted at Kirjath-jearim, threatened Beth-horon, and one column at least seemed headed straight for Gibeah.

Saul took the whole action as a personal affront, and was outraged. But David, seeing a chance to test his strike-force, was delighted. His men were mobilized within an hour after the news of the Philistine attack reached Gibeah. Saul would not let him move until larger columns under Jonathan and Abner were assembled. But David and his men were the first to set forth, wending their way down the valley of the Sorek, keeping to the shadowed slopes with advance patrols moving like antenna to find the enemy.

Saul had told David to move slowly and keep within sight of Jonathan's troops behind him. But once on the march, David was in no mood to imitate a mule train. He lost sight of Jonathan's troops around the second turn of the slopes and headed, he thought, for glory.

But what he marched into was an ambush. The rocks above seemed to bleed Philistines, who came pouring down the slope to push his troops down to the stream bed, where another contingent of Philistines suddenly appeared. Outnumbered, David and his men fought with youthful ferocity, hand-to-hand with the smooth-shaven men in feathered helmets. Joab took on three of them in sheer exuberance, eyes gleaming, sweat pouring down his face, his hand bloodied by an arm wound. David found the biggest Philistine in sight and flung himself into combat. In the thrust and parry of swords, the Philistine got a leg wound, and David got a clout on his helmet that cut his forehead and started blood streaming down his face. Abishai pulled him back and staunched the wound with a rakish tie of linen. David charged into the Philistines again.

In the fury of the fighting, David saw his treasured troops begin to wither before seasoned Philistine skill. Three of the hundred were dead, and the number of wounded were mounting. He could see fear and bewilderment in the eyes of some of his men as the Philistines pressed in, and the cries of battle grew shrill. David thought of retreat; he had to save his men. But, glancing over his shoulder, he saw the valley behind him filled with Hebrew troops surging forward. Jonathan's column engulfed David's men, shouldering them aside to reach the Philistines and forcing them, by sheer weight of numbers, down the valley until they broke and ran.

David was sitting on a rock, panting and mopping the blood and grime off his face, when he felt a hand on his shoulder. Turning, he saw Jonathan, standing behind him, the sunlight shining on his shield and helmet. He smiled at David. "You know, young man, it is not necessary for you to take on a whole Philistine army all by yourself."

David tried to act unfazed by the battle experience, but the sight of Jonathan was a wonder to his eyes, and the look of Jonathan warmed his soul.

Jonathan was as familiar to David as anyone in Saul's court, but suddenly in the valley of the Sorek there was a radiance about him like the morning sun on the wilderness hills of Judea. He felt a tingling consciousness of Jonathan's body, sheathed in sunlight, his hand still resting on David's shoulder. The bones and sinews of the hand were stark in their strength. Each hair on the back of the hand stood out in David's vision, the pores, the wrinkles around the knuckles, the even curves of the fingernails. He thought of the hand on his flesh and moved his shoulder gently beneath its pressure.

The hand withdrew.

Jonathan was never particularly impressed by David. True, he had a doglike, even touching, devotion to Saul and an effect on Saul that made the King considerably easier to deal with. But the youth himself exuded a kind of sanctimonious specialness that Jonathan and others in the court found irritating. What claim of grace did this shepherd-boy from Bethlehem have, except for Saul's favor? Surely, he curried that with almost sickening fidelity. And Saul sometimes seemed to sink to bathos in his response. But, in David, there was the aura of something more—an assurance that seemed bizarre in an untried youngster, but which had been evident ever since he had come to the court. No special favor of Saul had engendered it; he had brought it to Gibeah as casually as his clothing.

His brothers were ordinary enough, genial men with no pretensions. Jonathan wondered why they had not borne down on the youngest of the family to teach him their unassuming manner. But no. They, too, invested David with unworldly gifts. They, too, seemed to sense the aura—some pointed blessing from the Lord.

But what blessing? It was hard to see in David, as he followed Saul about in the field or played his harp in the royal tent at Gibeah, any touch of divine grace except his extraordinary beauty. Other youths might be handsome in a boyish way. But to Jonathan, David's beauty, no less virile, gleamed like the polish of precious stone—an abstract perfection, an incarnate imagining of the mind, beyond touch or passion. An embodiment of beauty fit only for a god or king.

That Saul enjoyed that embodiment, Jonathan had no

doubt. He had seen his father's eyes look on David with a searching hunger. He assumed that David sated that hunger with the seductiveness that Jonathan would occasionally glimpse just beneath the surface of his eyes. Glimpsing it, Jonathan would recoil. Not from David's maleness, but from the perfection that seemed too abstract to be wholly male—or even wholly human. Let the King cherish his booty from heaven. Jonathan would give himself to mortals.

What Jonathan had found in the valley of Sorek, bloodied, dirty, exhausted, and just faintly ridiculous, was a mortal. In that moment of recognition, the scales fell from his eyes. Jonathan loved David. Shaken by that recognition, Jonathan drew his hand away. He had felt the movement of the shoulder beneath his hand; he had caught the signal, and the signal had stirred exquisite tension in his groin. But David was Saul's.

David had recovered from the head wound he had gotten during the Philistine ambush when he met Jonathan one morning outside Saul's royal tent in Gibeah. Jonathan examined the scar and solemnly announced that he thought David would live. With a grin, David thanked him for his optimism. He basked in Jonathan's attention, the casual exchange between one commander and another, but he was tongue-tied for anything else to say. Jonathan saved him the trouble. "I know a wood not too far from here where there is game. Would you like to go hunting with me?"

"Yes," said David, "Yes." He could not disguise his eagerness.

Jonathan smiled. "Get your bow and a quiver of arrows. I'll meet you here shortly."

"I'll bring my sling, too," said David, and went off to his tent, his pulse racing, his mouth dry. All he feared was that Jonathan might have invited someone else to come along on the hunt.

125

But when he got back to the royal tent with quiver and bow slung over his shoulder, he found Jonathan waiting for him, alone.

Together they made their way from the rocky highlands of Gibeah to a forested valley on the slopes toward the Great Sea. David walked close beside Jonathan, matching his easy stride, until they entered the shaded coolness of the forest. Then David fell in line behind him as he wended his way through the trees and brush with an almost soundless prowl.

Jonathan shot a deer that day with his bow and arrow. David got two hares with his sling and nearly bagged a wandering Canaanite. But Jonathan dissuaded him. "We're after animals, David. Let the people go."

They cleaned their trophies in the stream and then sat down to drink from a skin of wine that Jonathan had brought and to eat some goat's milk cheese.

"I wish I had my harp here," said David. "I'd sing you a song."

Jonathan smiled at him. "You sing songs without a harp."

David was flustered. "What do you mean?"

"What you say . . . it has a way of singing."

David lowered his eyes. He shivered at the intimacy of Jonathan's voice, so poised, so casual. It seemed to envelop him as if David nestled in his arms. But he made no move. And Jonathan made no move toward him.

They went hunting several times that week. Each expedition was, for David, an exaltation and a torture. He was excruciatingly aware of every movement of Jonathan's body, every inflection of his voice, every flicker of expression on his face. He watched the play of sunlight on his hair, the corded muscles as he aimed an arrow, the glint in his eye as he searched the forest for the movement of game. The mere brush of his arm was searing to David's senses, and he ached to let his desire flood over Jonathan. But he knew he must wait upon the prince.

He felt the shadow of Saul between them. By gentle indirections David tried to make clear the implications of his new command. But perhaps the King's possession of him lingered like a fading aura. He chafed at the thought. His obsession with Jonathan seemed to blot out the past. Only Jonathan existed in the tender coils of his mind.

The early morning air was brisk when David and Jonathan left Gibeah for the forest, cloaks around their shoulders to fend off the chill. David had made a private, barely acknowledged resolve that he had waited long enough upon the Prince. This day the time would come when the unacted would be acted, the unspoken spoken. He sensed, not knowing how, an answering resolve in Jonathan. There was a nervousness between them—looks exchanged and avoided, arms brushing against each other, retreating.

David had never felt so exquisite a fear before, except perhaps when Samuel had looked at him. He felt in contact with some glory within himself beyond his consciousness or will. He was pulled toward the forest and his feet obeyed an unknown force. David walked without hesitation or qualms for he walked, he knew, in the sight of God. And that, too was a mystery. He would celebrate his own rite of revelation. In the act he would know more of his own nature.

Saul had been a titan to David, a giant of the earth, a lion in battle. David had loved him as he might love a great bear —to be attended to and cared for. In Saul he had found a tenderness that he had known only in his mother and father. David had been a child in his arms, a servant to the King's needs, a comforter of the Anointed.

But to Jonathan he would be neither child nor servant. He walked shoulder-to-shoulder with Jonathan, and could see in him the passage to his own maturity.

Deep in the forest they found a spring. The clear water of the pool shimmered in the dapple of sunlight that filtered through the boughs of cedar. Jonathan knelt by the pool, cupped the water in his hands and drank. David knelt close beside him and also drank. He saw their faces, reflected side-by-side in the quivering water. He turned and looked

127

at Jonathan. Their eyes met. With ritual solemnity, Jonathan reached up and held David's chin in his hand. He leaned forward and kissed him. David's lips responded. His hand moved around Jonathan's neck.

They rose to their feet and stood face-to-face in the clearing, their eyes caressing each other. Jonathan took his cloak from his shoulders and laid it on the ground as an offering to David. He put his bow and quiver by the cloak. He lay his belt and sword on the ground in front of David.

Clad only in their tunics, David and Jonathan stood silent their eyes never leaving each other. Then David loosened his tunic and let it fall to the ground. He stood naked before Jonathan. David lay down on Jonathan's cloak, and looked at the towering figure standing beside him. Jonathan took off his tunic. David felt his breath catch. He raised his arms. David's soul was knit with Jonathan's and he would celebrate it with his body.

David lay beside Saul in the field tent and thought about Jonathan. Saul was deep in sleep, but no sleep came to David. His mind dwelt on Jonathan's body—the hands, the arms, the shoulders, the cords of the neck. He ran his mind's fingers over each plane and angularity. He probed the crust of armor that encased the trunk of his body, lifting the plates to seek the animal substance beneath. He brushed against the hair of the legs and explored the bones of the knees, just above the bronze of the greaves. He wondered at the strength of the sandaled feet. Saul's body seemed dross beside it. But Saul must be cared for.

With stealth, David pulled back the coverlet and eased himself off the pallet where Saul lay sleeping. He slipped on his tunic and sandals, and, going outside the tent, shook the shoulder of Arad, who lay huddled and asleep under a cloak of Saul's.

Arad roused, his heavy-lidded eyes just visible in the moonlight.

"Stand up." David whispered the command.

Arad lurched to his feet, straightening his tunic as he did so.

David led him inside the tent, leaving the flap open for light. Arad stood shivering in the night chill.

"Take off your tunic."

Arad whined a protest. "It's *cold.*"

"I said take it off," David whispered. "You'll be warm soon enough."

Arad pulled his tunic over his head and dropped it to the floor of the tent. His naked body was shadowy in the shaft of moonlight, slender, almost fragile in its youth. He wrapped his arms around his bony chest and his teeth began to chatter. "What . . . are you . . . going to do with me?"

"Be still, and turn around."

Arad turned. The half-globes of his buttocks seemed opulent on his lean frame, firm with the tension of the cold, and smooth as a girl's. Saul, David thought with satisfaction, would be cared for. He reached over and took a cruet of fragrant oil, pouring some of it in his hand. "Bend over and spread your cheeks."

Arad whimpered. "What are you going . . ."

"You heard me."

Arad bent over. His hands reached his buttocks and the half-globes parted slightly. The hands, David noticed, were short-fingered, almost childlike.

"Now, hold still. You're going to be a good armor-bearer."

Arad gasped as David probed the crevice between his buttocks with oily fingers.

"Ow!"

"Be quiet. It will hurt worse if I don't do this."

Another whimper.

David's whisper grew gentle. "Relax. Let your muscles go."

"I can't . . ."

"For the King you can. Relax . . ."

In a pulsing silence, David felt the muscles yield. The

boy's hips slowly arched and David felt a grasping warmth. "That's right." David drew his hand away. "You will please the King."

"The King?" The whisper was almost a wail.

"Yes. The King." He steered the Arad's body to the pallet where Saul lay. "Now . . . very quietly lie down beside him. If you feel him press against you, relax. Just as you did with me. You understand? Relax, and hold still."

Arad was saucer-eyed as he nodded, and crept into bed beside Saul. David drew the coverlet over them both and left the tent.

David, feeling suddenly and wondrously free, wandered down to the stream of Sorek, and sat on its bank, watching the moonlight play on the ripples of the water. He knew that Jonathan was somewhere in the encampment, but he did not know where. No matter. He wanted to be alone with his fantasies. No place, time, or tie could impede their encircling union. Together they would find the vast waters of the Great Sea, the highlands of Bashan, and the mountain fastnesses of Phoenicia. They would exult in the stars. They would contemplate the mysteries of Egypt. No magnificence would be strange to them beyond the wonders of each other.

David flung himself full-length on the ground beside the stream as if to let the heavens descend on him. He imagined Jonathan above him, standing ghostlike beneath the trees, a Jonathan so transformed that he thought he had never seen him before.

He knew that no change had come to Jonathan's person. Only his eyes, as they had looked at him, had changed. All else was in his own vision, the unfolding of his own changing needs. When he had first come to Gibeah, a young stranger barely out of childhood, he had seen Saul as the strength of the earth, and he had needed to batten on that strength. But in the years of his maturing, as he had gathered Saul's strength to himself, he had grown fearful of the insistent impulses he felt that might threaten his tie to Saul. He no longer felt the pliant passivity of his first years with Saul—the passivity he had whispered so firmly to Arad, "Relax and hold still." David no longer wanted to hold still. He wanted the interplay of passionate companionship. He had tried to lure Saul into some new language of relationship. But Saul was old, and so accustomed to unassailable power that, despite some efforts, he faltered and fell back into his settled role. He was the King, and no mere companion to anyone, even in the dark privacy of embrace.

Since his whole life focused around Saul, David had grown lonely. He served not so much a man as a titan, monumental even in his most intimate moments of weakness. He knew that that titan was his special care, and the care was freely given. But the loneliness gnawed.

He had thought command might cure it. At least there would be some companionship of arms, however devoid of passion or even bodily contact. And indeed, young adventurers like Joab and Abishai had given him a zest for life that came most easily from his peers. But he felt no desire for either of them, nor for any among his men. Lonely as he was, he was still conditioned to Saul . . . until that moment when Jonathan was transformed in his vision.

David roused himself from the bank of the Sorek and walked back to Saul's tent. Raising the tent-flap, he peered in. Saul was asleep on his back. The boy was nestled beside him, one slender arm flung across Saul's chest. David felt a sudden wave of sadness. He could remember the surety of that great chest and how deeply he had needed that surety. His arm had been slender, too.

David lay down outside the tent, wrapped Saul's cloak around him, and huddled, as Arad had huddled, in the warmth of its folds. He guarded the King.

The yelp of pain was high-pitched and piercing, quickly followed by a sonorous grunt and roar. David reared up to

131

see Arad come lurching out of the tent, his naked body quivering, tears streaming down his face. He plunged under the cloak and clung to David, shaking with sobs.

He heard the thunderous voice inside the tent. "David! Where is David?"

Arad whispered in David's ear. "Don't go in there. Don't! It's terrible!"

David flared. "Saul is the King. He is terrible only to the enemies of the Lord. You are here to serve him."

"I tried. I tried . . . but . . ."

"You can and you will."

"DAVID!"

"Don't . . . !" Arad clutched him.

David twisted away and stood up. "I am here, my Lord."

"Come here, NOW!" The voice had a cutting anger.

David lifted the tent-flap and went into the tent. He could see Saul's eyes, big and flashing. "Where have you been?"

"I could not sleep, my Lord. I left you Arad."

Saul's tone was ominous. "When I want Arad, I will ask for Arad. Now . . . come to me."

Feeling chill to the marrow, David lay for the pleasure of the King. He held still, but he could not relax. The pain of Saul's entry was searing, and the anger of Saul's movements was crushing. For the first time since he had returned to Saul as "David of Bethlehem," he felt cruelly used, and felt his love for Saul betrayed. He was sickened with revulsion.

Only later did he take the measure of Saul's desperation.

Saul's anger was like a nightmare to David. His love for Jonathan made him powerless to respond to Saul and he walked through the inevitabilities with a trancelike fatalism. He would rather that Saul had flogged him senseless or have that one javelin thrust strike home. But no. He had to save himself for Jonathan's sake. So he must endure Saul's rages and his murderous designs, and, at the same time, the King's grotesque efforts to restore what had been lost to him.

David felt a bitter sadness one night in the field near

132

Hebron when, ensconced in his own commander's tent, he heard a bulllike grunting and rose to find Saul, standing and swaying outside his tent with Arad, frozen-eyed with fear, tugging at the King's tunic.

"David." Saul's voice was slurred and his face bloated with drunkenness. "Why are you here?" And he reached out a hand as if to gather David to himself. David could only think of a bear paw, heavy in its awkwardness, and, guiding it, wounded animal eyes. Looking at the spectacle, David wanted to take the man in his arms and cry on his shoulder. Yet, at the same time, he wanted to slap him to stir his addled brain, or even kill him to spare degradation to so mighty a king.

Instead, knowing Saul, David started talking to him softly and evenly. He could have been speaking Egyptian. Just the sound of his voice made Saul docile. David, with the help of Arad, led Saul back to the royal tent, where the big man collapsed on his pallet in a wine-drenched stupor. David sat beside Arad for a few moments, watching the breathing of the King, and then David went back to his own tent.

He knew that Saul's anger would follow his pleading, and David braced himself for the storms to come.

The first came at Gibeah. Late one afternoon, Ishbosheth came hurrying into the tent that he and David shared, shaking his head. "David, you had better go to Saul right away. You are the only one who can do anything with him when he gets in a mood like this."

"What has happened?"

Ishbosheth flung himself down on a leather cushion, his shoulders sloping abjectly. "It keeps getting worse. There is a demon in his spirit."

"What has he done?"

"He fought with Abner—they were shouting at each other and Abner stormed away. Then he insulted three Asherite elders and they left. He cursed Samuel to the high priests, yelled at the captain of the guard, and threatened to behead a dog that wandered into the tent. Nobody knows what to

133

do with him. You better go to him before he sunders Israel."

David felt a dull ache as he picked up his harp and went to the royal tent. What past could be evoke that would not fester the present? His mere self before the King might feed the storm. But what could he say to Ishbosheth? Regardless of his new command, to the court David was still Saul's sweet-voiced assuager. How could he say that he was the cause of the anger to be assuaged? What if he were to lay himself upon the ground before Saul's throne? He recoiled. He could not. From the very deeps of his soul, he could not. Yet the dull ache he felt was an ache for the anguish of Saul.

David entered the royal tent. Saul was sitting on his throne, a spear in his hand and a ferocious glower on his face. He barely acknowledged David's presence. David sat down some distance away from Saul and began to play soothing music on his harp—some of Saul's favorite pieces. But he could find no power of words to sign that would tell Saul how he felt and how he still loved the King. He hoped the music itself would speak to Saul; he put his heart into his fingers on the strings.

He kept watching Saul to see if some softening would come to his face, but, if anything, it seemed to harden as the eyes pierced the space between them, sharp as distant stars.

The arm raised, and in a flash, David saw the spear coming toward him. He twisted away and heard the spear whistle by. It buried itself in the rugs of the floor, the shaft still shaking.

David leapt to his feet. "No! It's not as you think! Please listen . . ."

But Saul reached for another spear. David fled the tent.

SEVEN

Absalom sat in the big chair, David's chair, Saul's chair, and enjoyed himself. Two Asherite harpists provided the music for nubile young dancers captured by his Judean contingent in a raid on the Moabites. Some were barely pubescent and moved with a childlike sensuality that Absalom found enticing.

With the exception of the youngest concubine, Yafa, who stood behind him and gently combed his hair, David's other concubines had been sent out of his sight. Absalom had thought of sending them to Philistine whorehouses. They had already served his purpose. The troops under his command now knew that Absalom was utterly committed to the rebellion, and they chafed, waiting for the signal to move against David and his troops in Gilead, to finish off what they had started.

But Absalom was enjoying himself. Jerusalem was sweet as honey from a comb, succulent as a ripened fig. He wanted to savor it. His taste for the opulent had been starved for a long time. Now he would sate his appetites.

He wore one of David's most resplendent robes—linen woven with strands of golden threads and fluted with Tyrian purple. He had seen David wear it, firmly gathered and high around the neck. But Absalom wore it loosely, his chest visible to the waist so that all might admire the grandeur of the royal person as much as the royal vestments.

He basked, languishing in his chair, watching the dancers glance at him as they turned their heads and bodies to the music. All he had to do was raise his hand and one of them would yield to royal lust. But he let his hand rest languidly on the arm of the chair. Royal favor would not be easily bestowed. So tantalizingly withheld, the blessing would be prized with wild abandon, clung to with piteous wiles. His eyes glided from body to body as the dancers whirled and undulated before him, their breasts and thighs molded under gossamer garments. Would it be the lithe little one with that vixen twinkle in her eye, or the fleshy child whose sultry somnolence he might awake to animal ferocity? He at first passed over the soulful-eyed girl who seemed to move with the trancelike resignation of a captive slave. Was she thinking of some mangy Moabite boy as she let the King's gaze rove her body? But Absalom returned to her as she swung by his chair, so distant and yet so close he nearly grabbed her. Ha! He'd soon make her forget any fleabitten Moabite! But he let his hand rest on the arm of the chair. Not yet. Not yet.

He thought, fleetingly, of how Amnon, as firstborn heir to David, expected to sit in the same chair. What a swine he would have been! He would have ravished at least three of the dancers in one sweaty entanglement, his pig eyes gleaming, his slack lips slavering, and his gross body straining for every last shred of pleasure. What a Canaanite debauch the court would have become!

But not with Absalom. No. He would fastidiously select those special women who would give him befitting adoration.

Amnon. Was David so blinded by the fact of birth? Oh, yes, Amnon had exuded a kind of brutish force, just like his mother, Ahinoam, so determined that *her* son would someday be the King. Didn't David understand what tyranny might have come to Israel? He would have made a whole nation of Tamars, raped and desolate, until the tribes of Jacob would have overthrown him and gone back to the chaos of the time of the Judges.

Absalom knew that his reign would have a happier fortune. David had spilled the blood. David had captured the trade routes. David had seized the land. David had gathered tribute. David had filled the royal coffers with gold. And Absalom would spend it. Absalom would build the Temple. Absalom would bring splendor to the tribes of Jacob, himself at the center, shining as the sun. The Lord, he knew, had willed his radiance.

Absalom raised his hand, and the Moabite captive was led to him. She stood before him, graceful as a fawn, but her eyes seemed to be focused on some mystery miles away. Absalom felt a flash of anger. He would make her look at him, just as thousands had looked at David when he had sat upon the throne.

He spoke to her sharply. "What is your name?"

"Luash." Her voice seemed listless.

"Moabite?"

"Edomite." But still the eyes wandered.

"Look at your King!"

Slowly her eyes focused on Absalom's face, but for all the light in them she could have been looking at a stone. He had seen that blank look before, passing him over while all attention focused on Amnon. But now he was on the throne and no mere Edomite girl was going to pass him by! If she would not look at him with adoration, he would see to it that she looked on him with fear and pleading. But she would look.

Absalom beckoned to Elon, his armor-bearer. "Take this girl to the royal chambers and guard her. I will be there shortly."

Elon bowed, and took the girl away. Absalom could see flickers of jealousy among the other dancers and he was warmed. Time enough for them after he had conquered

137

Edom. Then they would all know the devout attentions he expected.

When Absalom entered the royal chambers, he found the girl, Luash, standing in a corner, her shoulders hunched, her eyes downcast. Elon was sitting on the couch, polishing the leather on a pair of Absalom's sandals. The silence was thick. But Elon had done his tasks. The lamps were lit. The coverlet was turned down. The bowl of water and linens were in their place, and a curl of incense filled the room with fragrance. Absalom decided he would reward Elon by letting him take his pleasure on the girl after he was through with her.

But first . . . there was the girl.

Absalom looked at her distant passive figure and felt a sudden anger again. Didn't she know the wonder of her privilege? Did she think herself some whore-slave in Philistia? In the years of his exile from David's court, he had had some of them, and the experience was bitter in his memory. At Ashkelon or Gath he had been just another yokel Hebrew from the north country. What would they have said if he had told them he was son of David, the Great King? Then why aren't you at Jerusalem? And they would have laughed at him. So he had simply stood and taken his turn at Philistine or Egyptian bodies, spread out before him as unheeding as straw. Prince Absalom was a mule for such a manger!

He had raged at himself for his body's needs. He had raged at David for casting him out. He had raged at Amnon for shadowing him even in his death. But he had heaved and groaned in the straw, trying to find rest that would not come, trying to find response that was not there.

Now he was in the royal chambers and Luash was before him. Standing in the center of the room, he commanded her to come to him. She moved as if she were asleep until she was close to him, her head still downcast, and she stood motionless.

Straw!

138

Absalom glanced at Elon, fire in his eye, as if to signal him, and Elon quickly stiffened to attention, his boyish eyes gleaming as they followed Absalom's every move.

Absalom turned back to the girl and with one lashing motion stripped her of her tunic. She cried out and clutched her hands to her body.

Absalom grabbed her chin and pushed it upward. "Now . . . look at your King!"

Her eyes, awash with tears, seemed lost in watery deeps. She seemed as chill as a creature in the Great Sea.

Absalom turned away from her, his pulse racing, and anger gorged his throat. He had felt that anger before, and his struggle to control it had been the turmoil of his childhood. Now, faced with that vacant watery gaze that seemed to ignore his very presence, the anger surged through his whole body. The face of Luash was a thousand faces, stretching back into the desolations of his earliest memory where he saw the first of the faces—Amnon.

He swung back to the girl. His voice roared. "I AM HERE!"

Absalom put his robe back on, carefully adjusting the sleeves, the girdle, and the collar. He examined himself in the silver mirror. His beard, he decided, needed trimming above the lip. It was even growing a little long on the cheeks. He checked the wrinkles in his forehead, barely visible now, and hoped they would not grow any deeper. Still, though, a king should frown at the weight of his decisions. David had wrinkles. Perhaps he should cultivate them.

He combed his hair slowly, examining each side in the mirror to see that it had the proper gentle curl as it fell to his shoulders. He was reassured that his hairline was still as firm as ever, straight across his forehead. He was loath to contemplate the ravages of the years; he prayed himself exempt by the grandeur of his office, free from the bodily harms that festered in David. His would be a reign of

139

gentility. How could the children of Jacob expect any less from such a radiant king? The mirror told him this. The mirror was his reassurance. Eyes might pass him by, but the mirror told him he existed. He was Absalom, the King.

He smoothed his eyebrows, touched the curl of his hair again, and languished in the sweet calm of his perceptions. The calm always came when his anger was purged; now his subjects could bask in the fullness of its serenity.

He put down the mirror, and turned to view the scene upon the couch. The Edomite girl was still tied, wrists and ankles, with leather thongs. The welts on her torso were crimson, and blood seeped from the strip across her breasts. Elon, lithe and naked, was above her, the tension of his muscles etched in the lamplight as he thrust himself into her, one vicious stroke after another.

"When you are through, Elon, do not kill her," Absalom said. "She will be docile."

Absalom left the royal chambers and returned to the audience room.

Amasa, Absalom's military commander, was clipped in his announcement, but the grip he had on the sword hilt at his girdle betrayed his excitement. "A hundred have come from the tribe of Simeon—the first they have sent. Another two hundred Asherites are camped on the western hill. Talmai is marching in with a hundred Danites from Mount Hermon and they are expected here tomorrow."

Absalom glanced at Hushai. "They have come now from Dan to Beersheba."

Hushai nodded. "It is true."

"We have the strength now," Amasa measured his words, "to take the field, seek out David, and destroy him."

The three men sat around the table and looked at each other for a moment in silence. Absalom had sometimes had a fleeting hope that this moment would never come, that

140

he could continue to enjoy the sweetness of Jerusalem and the adulations of the throne while David aged, enfeebled, in Gilead. But the word had come to him that David, quartered at Mahanaim, was mustering his troops and drawing support from his allies across the Jordan. And David was a master of the surprise and crushing attack. To wait too long could be fatal. Still, he dreaded this moment, and he saw the dread in Hushai's eyes as well. But Amasa was determined. He was out to prove himself a better commander than Joab, and Absalom prayed that he was. But he was not sure. And now his life was in Amasa's hands.

"Show me your plan," Absalom said.

Amasa unrolled a map of papyrus, and spread it on the table. The three men hunched over the map as Amasa laid out his strategy, how the contingents would be divided, where the Jordan would be crossed, what supplies would be needed, where the attack would best be launched. It sounded reasonable to Absalom, and Hushai seemed impressed, but Absalom wondered what Joab would think of the plan or what lethal variations David himself might add. He knew how in the past the difference between defeat and victory had been spawned in David's head, nurtured by David's craft. But he did not know how David's mind had worked. He only knew the legend of David's prowess . . . and his guile.

How could he know more?

He could remember as a youth seeing his father and Joab hunched over a map, just as he was now with Amasa and Hushai. And who might be with them? Amnon, learning his princely lessons. Young Absalom would be gently dismissed from the room. If Amnon had died any other death, Absalom might have taken his place to learn what David had to teach. But, for Tamar's sake, Absalom had been driven into exile for the murder of Amnon. The exile from David he had felt as a child had become a physical fact. He could learn no more from David.

141

And now he was in Amasa's hands.

He turned to Hushai. Perhaps here was some reflected glimmering of David's mind. "What do you think?"

Hushai stroked his beard. "It is a sound plan. But even the soundest plans can go awry."

Amasa asked, "What do you mean?"

Hushai ran his finger over the map. "You'll be exposed fording the Jordan. You'll be exposed climbing that bluff. A sudden storm could flood that stream, or the well you are relying on here might have gone dry. There are risks . . ."

Amasa snorted. "There are risks in any battle."

"But you know as well as I do, Amasa, how clever David is at exploiting risks . . . other people's risks."

"You think he can stir a storm, or dry a well? Hushai, he may be anointed of the Lord, but he is not all that anointed!"

Absalom cut in. "Hushai, what would you suggest?"

"Time has passed since David fled. Tempers have cooled. I would be willing to go to David in Gilead as your emissary to work out . . ." Hushai held up his hands, ". . . some kind of arrangement."

Amasa slammed his hand down on the table. "Hushai, you prate!"

"Do I, Amasa?" Hushai's voice was ominously soft. "Once you cross the Jordan, the battle will be joined. And at the end of the battle one of two people will be dead. David, or Absalom. Father or son."

"Then it must be," said Absalom.

"It need not be."

"So what would you do? Go to David and plead with him to come and take his throne back?"

"The throne you would soon have anyway . . . if he forgives you."

"If he forgives me?" Absalom felt his anger boil. "If he forgives me! That man, that curse on my life. If *he* forgives *me*! At least he knows where to find me, now that I sit on his throne. Before he never knew. No. Amnon this. Amnon that. And who cared where Absalom was? All right! Let there be a battle, and let one of us be taken. And I'll tell you who, Hushai. David! I'll chase him down to the last pit in Manahaim and catch the old man crouching there." Absalom slapped his sword. "With one stroke, Hushai. One stroke and the curse is lifted!"

Absalom turned to Amasa. "We march tomorrow."

Hushai walked through the House of Cedar. He felt shaken by the rage he had seen in Absalom, the fineness of his face reddened and distorted as if by demons. He ached to think that David could have stirred such anger, and he feared what that anger might destroy.

He stopped at a doorway and entered a darkened room. Only the faintest shafts of daylight came through the crevices in the shutters, and he could hear no sound. He thought he sensed death.

"Mephibosheth?"

A silence.

"Mephibosheth?"

The voice was as faint as the light. "Yes."

"This is Hushai."

Another silence. Then Mephibosheth's voice came out of the darkness. "Have you come to kill me?"

"No. I have only come to see that you are all right."

"I am alive." A heavy sigh. "I guess he wants to keep me alive."

"Absalom?"

"Yes. But I do not wish to be alive. Not now."

"What happened? What did he do to you?"

"He always hated me."

"I know. He is full of hatred. But . . . ?" Hushai hesitated. He feared what he might hear. But he heard nothing.

"Mephibosheth . . ." Hushai's voice grew very gentle. "Tell me . . ."

"He raped me. He raped my mouth."

❖ ❖ ❖

143

Hushai walked out of the House of Cedar, his steps firm and steady. He passed the Tabernacle and went to the house of Zadok, the high priest. He spoke to Zadok softly. "I have information for the King concerning the battle plans of Absalom."

Zadok gave the information to a servant girl who passed out of the city gates unnoticed and went down the valley of Kidron to the Dragon's Spring. There she found Ahimaaz, Zadok's son, waiting for her. She gave the information to him. Ahimaaz rode his mule with all speed to David in Mahanaim.

David, with Joab beside him and a map in front of him, listened to Ahimaaz carefully. When he finished his report, David asked, "Will Absalom lead his troops?"

"I believe so."

David shook his head. "It would be better if he did not."

But Joab growled under his breath, "It will be good if he does." Once Ahimaaz left the room, David and Joab pored over the map, tracing the projected movement of Absalom's troops.

Finally David leaned back. "Typical of Amasa. Sound, but no originality."

"And relying on a rabble of troops from all over Israel," Joab added. "They'd as likely end up fighting each other."

David stared off into space, and he spoke dreamily. "Joab, do you remember the Forest of Ephraim?"

Joab shuddered. "Where God vented His wrath!"

"Do you suppose Amasa knows about the Forest of Ephraim?"

"Most of his campaigns were south, in Judea."

"But *we* know about the Forest of Ephraim, don't we, Joab?"

"Yes, my Lord, we do. Pits and potholes all covered with leaves and branches, and the forest itself so thick you can barely move. You'd fight a battle *there*?"

"Our troops are disciplined. Theirs are not. They would be susceptible to panic."

"How do we get them that far north?"

"We lure them, Joab. With great clouds of dust that would seem to signal troops in headlong flight, we lure them . . ."

". . . And then we turn on them."

David nodded.

Joab smiled. "I'll work out the details." Rolling up the map, he took his leave.

Alone, David brooded.

He could think of the battle to come and feel that pulse-quickening zest that had always come to him before a military challenge. He had tested himself, year after year, against the enemies of Israel, and each time felt his strength renewed.

But the battle looming now was not just a wily exercise in strategy, but a rending of his spirit. Whatever the outcome, he would lose flesh and blood—his own or Absalom's. The vision of Absalom being lost in the dank entanglements of the Forest of Ephraim—a very embodiment of Sheol—chilled him. He almost wished he had not thought of the wretched place. But confronted with Amasa's reported strategy, he had reacted as a warrior king, responsible for his troops and plotting to give them every advantage. And now the decision had been made. It seemed very natural with only Joab at his side. But what if Hushai had been there? Might he not have pointed out some chance to talk, some way to avert the lethal collision that Joab so relished? He wished for a moment that he had not sent Hushai back to Jerusalem. But then again, if he had not, he would not not know what he now knew and his troops might have been endangered by a horde of Israelites, led by a bloodthirsty Ahithophel. He had been well served by Hushai, and he prayed that Absalom would not find Hushai out. He had heard of Absalom's rages, the tantrums of a petulant child in the threatening body of a man. He feared for his hostages left in Jerusalem—Hushai, Mephibosheth, and Michal.

He thought ruefully of Michal, one of the wreckages in his life. He could remember the look in her eye, as resentful as Absalom's, just because he had taken her back as his queen instead of leaving her with that miserable farmer, Paltiel. Why hadn't she been grateful? True, the love between them had long since gone, but it had been there once. He had risked his life for her, raiding the Philistine encampment to get her bride-price. And she had risked her life for him, helping him escape Saul's murderous anger. But then? David had been in exile, with Saul and his army pursuing him all over the southern wildernesses while Michal had been kept at Gibeah. They had no chance. Still . . . he ached at the thought of Michal.

Saul. Another wreckage, bitterer still than Michal, because it had been his own doing. David sat in Mahanaim, facing battle with Absalom, and wondered how Saul had felt, encamped in the wilderness of Ziph, facing battle with young David. He could know now some of the anguish that Saul must have felt, but perhaps it had been deeper than what David now felt. David knew that Saul cared more about him than David cared about that vain, impetuous son of his. Absalom—and David bridled at the thought—was David's guilt. But young David had been Saul's emotional treasure, hoarded, guarded, and exulted in. Now he could know the loneliness of Saul and remember how, as a youth, he had assuaged it in a myriad of ways, but, at the same time, taking as his right all the emotional reassurance that Saul had to give. The erotic act was a symbol of all else; Saul, in his need, pouring himself into David's warmth, and David absorbing every last spasm not just as a gift of Saul's strength but a gift of his spirit. Through his tissues, he gathered Saul into himself. And Saul spent himself with desperate profligacy, grasping David in his arms so close he could hear the great heart beat, reaching the moment with his chest moving like belows, and falling back as if he had taken a mortal wound. David would cover him with his own body and sometimes fear that the last gift had been given. Then

Saul's eyes would open, big and warm. His hand would stroke David's hair. His arms would enwrap David's body. David would lie there in the hush and feel himself part of Saul.

Now, at Mahanaim, David brooded. The Philistines had finally defeated Saul at the battle of Gilboa. Saul and Jonathan had met again in Sheol. Would he and Absalom meet in Sheol after the battle of the Forest of Ephraim? And how would their souls mingle? He remembered the sharp jealousy when he had heard that both Saul and Jonathan had been killed. They would go to Sheol without him, father and son, as close as they had always been. But he and Absalom? What wars would they make with each other on the plains of heaven? Why had his fatherhood gone bitter while Saul's had been strong to the end?

His courtiers and the scribes never tired of telling David that he was a "Great King," blessed by the Lord as Saul had never been blessed, a man of empire while Saul had been little more than a tribal chieftain. And, yes, he knew it. But he knew more. Saul had Jonathan. But David was cursed with Absalom, and he was tortured with the suspicion that he had brought the curse upon himself, just as he had brought Saul's anger upon himself. The "Great King" knew himself better than the scribes, but he was vain enough to let them celebrate his public grandeur.

But what private grandeur could he rescue from the wreckages of his life? For once he could be magnanimous with Absalom. Yes. That. No need to war in Sheol. No need to splatter the afterlife with hatred. The wreckage could be repaired before the chance was gone. If Absalom lived. Yes, he must live. For himself, and to save David's life as well. Thus in his aging he would know a little grandeur in his own spirit, blessed with children who could give him filial love. And Absalom would be the crown of his fatherhood. Absalom must live.

147

He could envision the scene, deep in the gnarled mysteries of the Forest of Ephraim—Absalom's forces routed, Absalom himself captured. They would meet, warrior to warrior, king and prince. He could see Absalom standing, straight and defiant as David approached, waiting the stroke of the sword or the thrust of the spear. But David would hold up a restraining hand to his forces, and move forward to embrace Absalom, his son. Absalom would resist at first, his eyes flashing like a cornered lion's. But then he would see the warmth and magnanimity in David's eyes, and recognize the sincerity of David's gesture. He would be humbled to repentance for his rashness.

David and Absalom would walk out of the Forest of Ephraim together, united, father and son. All the Israelites and men of Judah would know that the house of Jacob was again one. But more. David would have purged himself of the anger that had corroded him during Absalom's exile. He would have laid the ghost of Amnon to rest. Yes, he could think of Absalom now, and know the anguish that must have beat upon him as he watched Tamar sicken. Why had he not taken justice into his own hands? Why had he not exiled Amnon after the rape of Tamar? Why had he waited until he was forced to exile Absalom after the murder of Amnon?

He thought about Amnon. The youth had seemed so shining to him, and his promise so infinite. To David, he had the strength of kingship. He could hold the empire together once David had forged it. Had his confidence been faulty, his vision distorted? Had the mere fact of fatherhood to a lusty youth made him blind to the possibility that the lusty youth was a swine?

Joab had never liked Amnon. He knew that. And Joab had pressed David to have Absalom returned from exile. Joab was a good judge of men. Did Joab think that Absalom in fact had the strength that David attributed to Amnon?

As David ruminated, another question suddenly filled his mind. He was so sure of victory against Absalom's ragged forces that he barely thought of defeat. But, in battle, anything was possible. What if it were David who stood before Absalom, captive and defiant? David quelled a visceral roar of outrage in his spirit. No arrogant youth would humble the King! Let the Lord smite him for his impudence! Never would he utter one word of obeisance; let the spear-thrust come first! Let an ungrateful Israel endure the anger of the Lord for betraying its anointed.

Then David thought of Saul. It had not been quite so, thirty-five years before in the wilderness of Ziph. Young David had not captured Saul, but he had humbled him with the seizure of the royal spear and water jar. They had talked. Saul had said, love and despair in his eyes, "I have done wrong. Come back, David, my son."

What he had learned, he had learned from Saul. The arts of killing were Saul's arts, and David had followed the master as he bestrode the hills. David had wondered at the man's casual power, the easy course of his movements, the stolid rhythm of his march, and the relaxation of his resting. The field was his home and he languished there till the enemy was sighted, the ram's horn sounded. Then the power in him flowed like a torrent, sweeping his men into battle.

He had felt Saul's power flow into him, and he had gathered it to himself. As his youthful strength grew, he tested himself to vie with the source. And Saul, with what seemed at first a confident assurance, gave him troops, gave him commands, gave him the very substance with which he could strain his own power to its limits. In campaign after campaign against the Philistines, David had come to know the vibrancy of public adulation. Returning from battle to Gibeah, David had seen the women dancing with tambourines, heard them as they made merry singing

> Saul made havoc among thousands,
> but David among tens of thousands.

149

He knew they were only taken with the freshness of his youth, and that Saul remained the mightiest warrior of Israel and Judah. But he loved the sound of those women's voices. Yet when Michal, Saul's young daughter, had repeated the doggerel, he had clamped his hand over her mouth. "Don't let your father ever hear you sing that!" But she had given him a mischievous look, and went on her way, humming the tune.

Saul's eyes were more hooded than ever. No gesture, word, or kindness that David would offer could break through the facade of stern impassivity that Saul showed to David. Only sudden outbursts of frenzy betrayed the depths of Saul's enmity, and no gentle words from Jonathan could assuage David's fear of it.

But there was Michal. If Jonathan had led to the rift between David and Saul, perhaps Michal might heal it, and keep David within the graces of the royal house. It was a slender girl on whom David placed a heavy hope. But she loved him; he knew that. And she was Jonathan's flesh and blood. She was one more way in which David could be closer to him.

He turned his charm on her. She must have thought it strange. He had been at the court three years; first his attention had focused on Saul, then on Jonathan. Michal to him had been only a presence, looking at him with adoring eyes, but he was used to that. His intimacy with the King gave luster to his growing youthful beauty, and the eyes of the young women of the court were attentive, the more so since he seemed quite unattainable.

Now, endangered at court, David saw Michal in a new light. She was not particularly attractive; no one could rival Jonathan's grandeur—the cast of his head, the hardness of his body. But her body was lean, almost boyish; her eyes were warm; and, caught in David's charm, she responded with a gentle playfulness. Did her coquetry mask her doubt? Now in pursuit, David was determined to overcome it. In

150

every move, he sought to convince her of his sudden devotion. She was still young. It was not difficult.

One evening, Saul's court assembled in the royal tent at Gibeah, and David, now commander of troops, had eased himself down next to Michal for the harp-playing and dancing that it was Saul's pleasure to have after the evening meal. Arad, the harpist, was about the age that David had been when he had first come from Bethlehem. He sat close by Saul's feet as the King lounged in his big chair, a hand resting on the harpist's shoulder as he played.

David felt a twinge of jealousy. He remembered how that hand felt, the assurance of being safe by the King's side, the warmth so casually bestowed. But David was no longer there; he felt no assurance, only anxiety at the occasional glowers that Saul cast in his direction. He wondered how it fared with Arad. Was Saul using him as he had used David? If so, did the boy know his power, and the danger of that power? David could tell him—oh, yes—but he never would. Let the boy work out his own course.

The dancer was a lissome Ammonite girl, barely beyond childhood, whom Saul had selected as one of his concubines. Dressed in a scanty tunic, artfully cut and revealing, she moved to the music, tinkling her finger-cymbals to the rhythm. On her lips was a childlike pout. Her eyes scanned the ceiling of the tent. But her body thrust itself toward the throne with wanton insistence, beat after beat, while Saul slouched inert in his chair, his hand still on Arad's shoulder.

David looked across the room and saw Ishbosheth, gawking at the throbbings of the Ammonite dancer, a fleck of saliva on his lower lip. Ishbosheth's eyes deflected to David's, a lecherous grin on his face. David winked. Ishbosheth winked, glanced at Saul on the throne, and shook his head. David shrugged, and moved closer to Michal. His groin was stirred by the dancer's writhings, and in the lamplight, Michal looked almost beautiful.

151

The music and the dancing ended, and Saul was distracted by some counselors huddled around the throne. David grasped Michal by the hand and led her out of the tent, into the night and the blazing starlight. A cool breeze blew off the Great Sea, wafting away the heat and stench of the day. The earth seemed clean again, washed in a tide of night air stealthy as a flow of water.

David felt fresh after the close odors of food, wine, and bodies in the tent. Even Michal seemed transformed in the darkness. Her identity, her entanglements, her very royalty were dimmed and the presence beside him seemed as impersonally seductive as the Ammonite dancer.

He led her by the hand—she followed unquestioningly— to a rise of ground above the encampment at Gibeah, sheltered from the west wind by a grove of cedars. They sat on the soft earth and watched the flicker of torchlights moving among the tents of Gibeah. On other hills, they saw the campfires of shepherds who had settled their flocks for the night, and heard the bark and howl of sheepdogs, defying the dark.

Michal sat close to him. David's thoughts glided over the situation as easily as his arm enwrapped her waist. In the plethora of his sexual images, he could find lust for her— no burgeoning exaltation, but an occasional domestic desire suitable to polygamous matrimony. And she would be grateful. She could be herded for his purpose, but with a gentle guidance. No sling. No stick. No dog. Only his touch and the caress of his eyes.

Saul would look at him again. His eyes not hooded, but big and proud. He would feel that bearlike arm on his shoulder, and the warmth of his hand. David would be son-in-law to the king. Favored like Jonathan. He might even bring favor to Ishbosheth. He cared about that. He had come to know how Ishbosheth felt in the court; they had shared the wink of outcasts. But now the King's daughter was beside him. Through her—he barely allowed himself the thought—the royal line might pass to the house of David.

David pointed across to one of the hills where the shepherds rested with their flocks. "My dog used to bark like that. I'd settle down under my robe for the night, and suddenly, he'd start, raising an uproar about some locust or hare in the bush, and I'd be up with my sling, ready for a bear or lion stalking the flock. And there would be nothing. Just that dog noising up the night air, and the sheep all huddled with fear."

Michal said, "You were a good shepherd."

"A good shepherd is always scared himself. He shares his fear with the sheep. But that dog . . . oh, I got used to him. He'd start to bark, and I'd just lie there under my robe, waiting for the locust to fly away, the hare to run, his imaginings of the night to vanish. And mostly, he'd stop. But one time he didn't. It was clear, like tonight, with only starlight. His barking grew hard and shrill. Then I heard the sound. The low growl. I knew it wasn't a hare in the bush. Something big was out there in the darkness. The flock knew it, too, and their bleats mingled with the dog's barking. I lay there, under my robe, my heart beating hard. I knew I had to get up. I knew the flock was in danger. But it was danger for me, too. I wanted to hide. I wanted to run. But how could I eat at my father's table if sheep were lost?

"I crawled out from under the robe, and gathered some stones for my sling. I moved around the flock, coming close to where the dog was barking. Then I saw it, a ghost, a spirit almost, lurking, just visible out there beyond the firelight. I knew the stealth and the slink of it. It was a lion. It would crouch soon, and in a rush, crunch the neck of one of the lambs. Or would it be the dog? Or would it be me?

"I put a stone in my sling as I saw the lion's eyes glow in the darkness. I took aim, and let the stone fly, afraid that it would only whet his rage for blood. But the stone struck true. I heard a yelp of pain, and then the body crashing through the brush. I did not sleep that night. I knew it might come back."

David stretched back on the earth beside Michal, his eyes scanning the stars. "Strange. I used to dream about that lion. Its eyes would grow sharp as starlight, fixing its gleam on me, as if it pinioned me to the earth so I could be ravaged like a carcass. I could feel its breath as the eyes held me, the warmth of its smoothly haired flesh, and finally the rake of its claws as it tore me apart. The lion. Sometimes I thought its face was like the face of God. Sometimes like Saul's . . ."

Michal put her hand on his arm. "But Saul loves you. It is only . . . only that he is proud."

"But what have I done?" He tried to keep the falsity out of his voice. "I have served him. I played the harp for him to quiet his spirit. I bore his armor to the battle. I led his troops against the Philistines and won victories for Israel. Still he is angry with me as if my loyalty were some cursed thing. What have I done? Why is his favor so fickle?"

Michal was silent for a moment. Then she sighed. "You men are so mysterious. How are women supposed to cope with all these squalls and tempers that seem to come and go like the shifting wind? I look at you, David. Even you, with all the world before you. But if Saul glowers at you, you brood for hours. If Jonathan does not hail you in just the right tone, you are like a whipped dog. And you and Ishbosheth . . . I think you speak Egyptian to each other for all I can understand of it. And here I've been for years, prancing and dancing, looking at you with calf's eyes, swinging from the tree tops . . . anything, just to make you see me. But no. You're a man . . . a big mysterious man . . ."

"I see you now."

"The wonder of it!" She laughed lightly. "I must have conjured up a spirit to turn your eyes!"

"They have always seen you." He put a hand on her shoulder. "Come, lie beside me and watch the stars."

She made no move. "What have the stars to tell me?"

"Many things, perhaps. The Philistines, it is said, guide

their ships by the stars. The Egyptians claim they foretell the future . . ."

"Such things belong to the Lord."

"But if He moves the stars across the heavens . . ." David's voice grew soft, ". . . maybe we can read His Will." He pointed to the horizon. "See, the bright one is rising . . . and there, beside it, another, almost as bright. They seem joined together as they climb in the sky."

"You do not know."

"I have watched many nights, alone with the flock in the hills. They will rise together."

"It seems a sorcery to think about," she said, but she finally lay down beside him. "They are only stars."

He stroked her hair with his hand. "The Egyptians know many things."

She stared straight above her. "So lonely, there in the blackness."

"But the stars keep each other company, hanging there in the sky."

"Do you think they talk to each other?"

"Yes. I've never heard them. But I don't think the Lord would make beings who could not speak and tell each other the moods of their spirits."

"I wonder what they say."

"Oh, probably the same things we say to each other on earth. They draw close, and keep each other warm, and wonder how it is on the great flat deserts of the world. Maybe they do not know that we are watching them, too."

Michal nestled close. "We'll hide so they won't see us."

David put his arm under her head. "It would not do to have them spying on us." He shuddered slightly. "Worse than Saul."

Michal raised herself on one elbow. "There you go again, fretting about Saul!" She brushed a hand against his cheek. "Why must he be with us, even here?"

David's voice was measured. "If our stars are to rise together, Saul must order the sky."

Michal put her head on his shoulder. After a long silence she spoke in a voice as solemn as David's. "I will speak to my father."

Now it was David's turn to watch Michal. He followed her with his eyes whenever he saw her around the court. Had she spoken to Saul? Or was she waiting? What was she waiting for? Or had Saul rejected her and was she biding her time to catch him in a more yielding mood? He scanned her looks, her stance, her voice, for some clue. But she was only sweet and noncommittal. And days passed. He tried to get her alone to ask her, but she eluded him. He feared that his last hope of favor in the court was vanishing, and he would soon be on his way back to Bethlehem in exile, cut off from Jonathan, stripped of power, destined to live out his life in the rhythms of the farming seasons.

He had been happy enough in Bethlehem, but three years in Saul's court had made Bethlehem seem dull. Returning now would be a little death. The very thought of sheep made him ill.

Five days passed without David's hearing a word from anyone. Then, after evening meal, Abner, Saul's commander, invited David to his tent. As he walked the short paces from the royal tent to Abner's, David was in turmoil. Abner was Saul's right arm. Was that arm to kill him for the King's pleasure? Or was Abner simply planning another foray against the Philistines and going to give David and his contingent a part in that action?

He entered the tent and found Abner alone. No armor-bearer or servant was anywhere in sight. Abner himself wore no armor, only a simple tunic, and no weapons dangled at his waist. If Abner was going to kill him, he seemed ill prepared, and David relaxed . . . a little. But the way Abner looked at him—with an impassive steady stare—David still

156

wasn't entirely sure that he was going to get out of the tent alive.

Abner gestured to a high cushion of skins and poured David a cup of wine. He sat down on another cushion and nursed his own wine cup, surveying David over its rim. "You've grown, David."

"It happens to us all."

"Yes, but I did not think you would grow to such a stature."

David looked at himself in puzzlement. He was a little over medium height, but Saul and Abner still towered over him. "What do you mean?"

"When you first came from Bethlehem, you were not . . ." Abner hesitated and his eyes warmed, ". . . very impressive. A boy. A callow boy. With a certain charm, I suppose, but only Saul seemed to realize it. I hoped that you would grow up like your brothers, but it seemed unlikely."

David grinned. It was a tentative grin, but the conversation did not seem to be leading to assassination.

"But now I see that you have the makings of a mighty warrior. You can lead men, young as you are. You attend to the small things as well as the big things. A lot of war is small things. And you have a precious guile, the stuff of ambush and surprise. Oh, yes, the Philistines will regret that you ever left your sheep!"

"Thank you, my Lord. All I want is the favor of the King."

Abner heaved a great sigh, and emptied his wine cup. He set it down on a small table beside him. Then he gave forth with a rumbling belch, staring at the roof of the tent as he did so. " 'The favor of the King,' indeed. I have served Saul for the years of his kingship. We have planned. We have plotted. We have led the troops and we have fought shoulder-to-shoulder. But know 'the favor of the King'? Ha! His mind . . . sometimes it charges like a wild bull . . . sometimes it scurries through the brush like a fox . . . and sometimes it slithers through the rocks like a serpent. I look at him and I think . . . what am I looking at? A bull? A

157

fox? Or a serpent? Most people see only the bull. That is why they do not understand him. But you, you were his armor-bearer. You knew his every movement, had his every favor. What did you see?"

"A bull. A fox. A serpent. All those." David felt his eyes fill up. "But I loved a man."

The tent was silent as Abner helped himself to another cup of wine. His voice grew mournful. "Such things happen. Their strength is their danger. Still, even now, the King is well disposed to you."

"He told you that?"

"He spoke it to me."

"But what he speaks . . ."

Abner shrugged. ". . . Is sometimes what is on his mind, and sometimes not."

"Tell me what he said."

"He said that it is time for you to marry into the King's family. Since he has only one unmarried daughter now, I take it that you will marry Michal."

David did his best to feign consternation. "Michal? I . . . marry the King's daughter?"

Abner nodded. "That seems to be his wish."

"But I am a farmer's son from Bethlehem, someone of no consequence."

"Come, David," Abner snorted. "Try modesty on sweeter souls than me. I know somewhere in your secret self you feel chosen by the Lord, and that Michal is your rightful due. You have, after all, been . . ." a faint smile crossed Abner's face, ". . . most intimate with the house of Saul."

David felt panic. How much did Abner know?

But Abner quickly covered with the flow of his talk. "You should know, however, that the King demands a bride-price."

"A price? But I have nothing!" David thought for a moment. "Still, I could lead a raid. I could find booty . . ."

"He asks booty . . . of a sort."

"What sort?"

"A hundred Philistine foreskins."

"For Michal? For the King's favor? I would bring him two hundred foreskins!"

Abner raised his hand. The scars of battle past showed his forearm. "David, sometimes your youth betrays you."

"Still . . . I could do it!"

"Perhaps you can. But perhaps it might be the Philistines who get the booty—your head! It might cause joy, impaled on a gatepost in Gath. It might even cause joy in Gibeah."

"What do you mean? The King is well disposed to me. You said that."

"Indeed. As it was said to me. But if I had a serpent mind, and wanted to get rid of a future son-in-law and rival, what better than to send him, all panting with youthful enthusiasm, on a risky raid against the Philistines?"

"But if I brought the foreskins back . . . ?"

"Yes. He would keep his word. You would be the King's son-in-law."

David paused, and thought some guileful thoughts. "I will go, then."

For the first time in their talk, Abner smiled. "Then, my young warrior, you had better listen to me."

"Tell me."

With deliberate movements, Abner put a goatskin on the floor between them, skin side up. He poked around the tent until he found a charcoaled stick. He waved it in front of David. "Saul and I planned many campaigns with sticks like this. Now, hear me well."

David bent over the goatskin as Abner drew a circle at one end of it. "Now, there's Ekron. The Philistines hold it." He drew a line out of the circle. "This is the road to Aijalon in Judea. Halfway up that road, about here . . ." he drew an X on the line, ". . . there is a Philistine outpost. Fortified. About a thousand men. Now, here's a stream. And here's a stream. And here's a hill covered with trees . . ." The stick moved rapidly over the goat skin.

Abner looked at David and his eyes had a predatory

gleam. "Two days from now, there is going to be a festival to their god Dagon all over Philistia—including this encampment. Much wine will be drunk. The night patrols will be sleepy . . ." Abner talked on. David listened intently.

Saul, in the royal tent, drowsed in satisfaction. The thorn would soon be pulled from his side. David would be dead. Still, he felt a dull ache, remembering the boy who had come from Bethlehem. He recalled that boy, lying on a pallet, his arms outstretched.

David crawled through the underbrush of the forest on the hill on the Ekron road. He and the troops around him moved stealthily in the darkness, but he could hear soft bird whistles to the right and left as the contingents signaled their locations. He wished Abner were with him, but he was grateful for the memory of the rasping voice that had given him instructions for the whole action as he had stared at the goat skin.

Glimpsing the encampment below on the other side of the Ekron road as he peered through the trees, David prayed that the festival for Dagon had been a debauch and that the troops lay wine-soaked in the night. He saw no patrols; he heard no sound coming from the encampment. He felt uneasy. Had some word of the raid gotten to the Philistines? Were they waiting, awake and fully armed behind the walls, for the Israelites to strike?

On the edge of the sharp incline down to the road, still hidden in the brush, David saw the gates of the encampment slowly swing open. The ruse had worked. David checked his pouch. His fingers touched the long skein of linen string with the sharp bone needle at the end. His pulse pounding in his throat, David gave a staccato whistle, and heard it answered from left and right. The troops poured down the incline, crossed the road, and swept through the

160

open gate with muffled movements into the Philistine encampment.

Like ghosts, the Israelites stalked down the pathways of the camp and disappeared into tent after tent filled with sleeping Philistines. Soon the air was filled with the shrieks and grunts of human agony as David's men went about their slaughter. Then the men, one by one, came back to David, bits of skin in their hands. Carefully David impaled each piece of skin on the needle and pushed it down the length of the linen skein.

The Philistines aroused, the slaughter turned into a battle with the half-clad men from Ekron and Gath wielding their iron swords, smiting the Hebrews, and drawing blood. Soon the grunts and wails were coming from David's troops as well as the Philistines. A skirmish swirled around David, who stuffed the string of flesh into his pouch and grabbed his sword as a young Philistine—barely an armor-bearer—made a lunge for him. David deflected the blow and struck back. The boy fell, blood streaming down his face. David was on him, pulled back his tunic, and found the flesh he wanted. The boy screamed. David stretched the flesh and with his bronze sword hacked it off. The boy gibbered with pain. David stuck his sword in the boy's throat to silence him, and turned to meet another Philistine coming at him with his sword swinging toward David's head. He saw the fury in the man's eyes, but he dodged the blow, and one of his guards finished the man with a thrust to the gut. Two more skins were needled onto the string.

Retreating as swiftly as they had come, David and his troops were soon safe again in the forest on the hill. David gave thanks to the Lord who had delivered him from the hands of the Philistines.

David marched with his troops into Gibeah late the following afternoon. Abner and his guards met him at the edge of the town. Abner looked at David quizzically, but David embraced him. "I did it as you told me to." He pointed to his pouch and smiled.

Abner shook his head and clapped David on the shoulder. "You are truly the blessed of Israel." He led David and his troops toward the royal tent.

Cretan mercenaries were standing guard outside the tent. David saluted the captain. "I have a gift for the King."

The captain disappeared inside the tent and returned in a few moments. "The King will see you."

David entered the tent, the pouch dangling at his side. Saul sat on his chair, attended by some of the elders of Judah, who scrutinized the young man from Bethlehem with care as one of their own tribe. David straightened as he saw them and stepped toward the throne with princely aplomb. He bowed formally to Saul and, detaching the pouch from his belt, said, "I bring you, my Lord, the bride-price for Michal." He placed the pouch on a table before the throne.

Saul looked at David warily, and then at the pouch. "You have brought me what I asked?"

"Double what you asked." David said. "Two hundred Philistine foreskins."

Saul picked up the pouch, opened it, peered inside. Then he handed the pouch to a guard. "Count them."

The guard froze, then held out his hand slowly and took the pouch. He pulled out the string of bloody flesh, his hand shaking as he did so, and started to count, his fingers moving from one bit of flesh to the next.

"Keep counting," Saul commanded.

He counted two hundred and six.

Saul rose from his chair, a grudging smile on his face. "You are a brave man, David. I am well pleased with you, and you shall be a member of the King's family." And he put his arm around David's shoulder. David basked in the warmth of it. The Judean elders spoke proudly among themselves.

❧   ❧   ❧

He had brought her to his chambers in a house in Gibeah, provided by Saul. Ishbosheth had wished him well and brought to the wedding ceremony a goatskin of fine Carmel wine. Saul had stood, glowing, as the high priest had performed the ceremony. Jonathan . . . oh, Jonathan! . . . had stood beside Saul, and pressed his hand to David's when the ceremony was done. David had taken Michal to the chambers.

She was everything to him. Saul. Jonathan. And her own self. And, through the slaughter of the Philistines, he was triumphant among the children of Jacob. David was a prince, his favor in the court impregnable.

Within the chambers, he drew her into his arms. So he would savor another special closeness to the King, in her womanly being. No rigors of maleness nor thunders of aggression. He could be lost in the gentle sea of her.

But she held back. Her lips tightened. Her eyes filled with fear. She held back. And no blandishments of David could bring her yielding. In the lamplight, her hair falling to her shoulders, her robe parted, she spoke the words, "Go, or tomorrow you will be dead." She kissed every part of him and then guided him to the window. Again, David fled from Saul.

Joab sat beside David on a hillside in the wilderness of Judea, two youths in exile from Saul's court. He flipped a pebble down the slope and put the question to David. "What does that crazy man think he is doing?"

"The Lord's anointed," said David, "has come to kill me."

Joab snorted. "A thousand of the best troops of Jacob say he won't."

"Perhaps it would be better if he did."

"I know . . . I know . . . Every time you threaten to leave for Sheol, we win another victory. Tell me, David, what fierce stratagems do you glean from flirtations with your own demise?"

David arched one eyebrow. "The willingness to gamble."

Joab grinned. "If I follow you to Sheol, we'll never get there."

"But now . . . no victory."

Joab exploded. "The man is mad!"

"He is my King, and I love him."

This time, Joab threw a rock that bounded down the parched slope. Whereupon he sat, breathing hard and saying nothing. When he spoke, his words came slow. "Let him camp with his horde. Come nightfall, Abishai and I will bring you his head."

David spoke as slowly. "This is my command, Joab. And Saul is my King. No hair on his head will be taken. No drop of his blood will be spilled." David hesitated. "But still . . . Joab . . . perhaps . . ."

Joab looked at David from beneath his brow "My Lord, what have you in mind?"

A thin new moon was high in the heavens. A wind off the great sea stirred eddies of dust as David and Abishai, cloaks over their armor and their helmets down over their foreheads, made their cautious way to the encampment of Saul and his troops. They saluted a sleepy night patrolman at the edge of the camp and moved with casual deliberation into the camp, wending their path through rows of tents and sleeping bodies lying on the ground, their cloaks wrapped around them. Some would occasionally stir and look at the two passing men, but their dress was like any other in Saul's army, their beards as bristling, their gait as steady. The sleepers would hunch up in their cloaks to sleep again.

The spear was planted upright outside the tent. Its polished bronze tip had a faint glint as it pointed, sharp, to the night sky. The spear marked the royal tent. David and Abishai slowed their steps when they saw it. Abishai whispered. "Let me . . . Just one thrust of that spear. Just one thrust . . ."

164

"No," said David. "Only take the spear. Do not use it."

They approached the tent, walking stealthily through the sand. Abishai grasped the spear and pulled it out of the ground. Gesturing to Abishai to stay where he was, David pulled back the flap and entered the tent. He saw Saul's great body asleep, and barely visible beside him, the slim body of Arad. David smiled to himself. Saul's rage at David could not overcome the habits of the night, or the comforts of a boy's body. Still, David was glad to think that Arad had finally learned how to relax.

David stood for a moment, contemplating that strange defenseless pair, and wondering what fate would come to Arad.

Slowly David leaned down to the head of Saul's pallet, picked up Saul's water jar, and left the tent. Carrying both spear and water jar, David and Abishai left Saul's encampment as discreetly as they had come, and only when they were far out of hearing distance did Abishai burst out laughing. "I just want to look on Saul and Abner's face in the morning!"

David gave an answering grin, swinging the water jar as he did so. But then his face darkened. "Still . . . it was a solemn matter."

"Oh, I'm sure . . . I'm sure. But, ha! I'd like to see someone try to steal *my* water jar!"

At dawn that morning, David and Abishai stood on a slope overlooking Saul's encampment, attended by guards. Abishai held the spear. David held the water jar.

David spoke in a loud voice. "Abner! Abner! Are you awake?"

Some moments of silence. Then Abner's voice boomed. "Who are you?"

Abishai chimed in. "How was the wine last night, Abner?"

Abner appeared at the edge of the encampment, buckling on his sword. "Oh . . . David . . ."

David spoke. "Did you guard the King last night?"

"Of course I guarded the King!"

165

"Then where is the King's spear? And where is his water jar that was at his head when he slept?"

Saul appeared beside Abner. "David, my son."

"I am here," said David. "With your spear and water jar."

Saul started to walk toward David. Abner began to follow him but Saul gestured him back. David took the spear from Abishai, and started down the slope toward Saul.

Saul walked heavily and his shoulders seemed to bear great weight. But David approached warily. Saul could feign weariness, and then strike like a bear. David held the spear in a strong grasp, its bronze head, flashing in the sunlight, pointed at Saul. But Saul wore only armor. He carried no weapon. And his arms were easy at his sides. Still . . . even his bare hands could be crushing.

When David grew close enough to see Saul's eyes, he knew that of all the battling elements within Saul's soul, the one that now commanded him was remorse. What else might command him at another hour, he could not know. But now . . . a tired regret as poignant as any that David had felt for Saul.

Eye to eye, an arm's reach from the King, David planted the spear in the ground, and put the water jar at Saul's feet. All he had felt for Saul suddenly came welling up within him. He embraced the King. Saul cradled David's head in his arms. His voice cracked when he spoke. "I have done wrong. Come back, David, my son."

David kissed Saul, and then gently pushed himself away. He turned and walked back up the slope to his own men.

It was the last time that David saw Saul.

Saul stood on the slopes of Mount Gilboa and watched Abner's line, below him in the Valley of Jezreel, being savaged by Philistine chariots. He ached to be in the midst of the battle, but his hair was white now; his joints were stiff; and his commanders feared his capture and humiliation at the hands of the Philistines. Saul stood with his armor-bearer, Arad, and a tattered collection of reserves. His eyes watered at the bleeding of Israel.

Still, there was Jonathan. He could see the glint of armor up the valley, moving fast. Jonathan was leading reinforcements from Beth-shean to relieve Abner's embattled forces. As the troops from Beth-shean moved nearer, the white of Jonathan's plumed helmet was visible.

Arad, standing close to the old King, murmured, "Now it will turn, my Lord. Now it will turn."

Abner's troops pulled back and regrouped on the slopes of Gilboa where the Philistine chariots could not maneuver. But Abner was followed not only by Philistine foot-soldiers but by a company of archers, who kept hailing the Israelites with high-flying iron-tipped arrows that could pierce the bronze plate armor of the Israelites.

The Philistine chariots thundered on at full gallop up the Valley of Jezreel to meet Jonathan's troops. As the chariots drew close, Jonathan's column took formation, shoulder-to-shoulder, spears in hand, and, at a shouted order, flung the spears at the oncoming horses. The attack was broken in a carnage of stumbling, flailing horses' bodies. But another wave of chariots wheeled around either flank of the formation, and it began to crumble in a chaos of combat.

Saul strained his eyes for a sight of Jonathan's plume, but he could not see it in the dust of battle. In desperation he shouted orders to his reserves to descend the slopes of Gilboa to rescue Jonathan. But the Philistine archers caught sight of Saul's forces on the move, turned from their attack on Abner's troops, and aimed their arrows at Saul's.

Saul was breathing heavily as he made his ponderous way down the slope, Arad holding his arm to steady him. His eyes were so focused on the battle in the valley that he barely watched where he was stepping. Suddenly he felt a lightning pain in his gut, stumbled, and fell like a great oak.

Arad eased his body over until Saul sat upon the ground, almost stifled with pain, a Philistine arrow sticking out from his armor. "Arad! Tell them to go forward!"

167

Arad motioned the troops to keep going down the slope. As they went by, they looked at the King, astonished that he now seemed mortal. But Saul did not notice them. His eyes combed the distance for Jonathan's white plume.

And then he saw it, standing high in the midst of a formation of Hebrews who were frantically fending off the swoop of Philistine chariots. He saw Jonathan and a few others suddenly break from the formation, and with spear thrust and sword stroke, try to fell the horse of one of the chariots. The horse reared and trampled one of Jonathan's companions. Jonathan attacked the man in the chariot, but the Philistine, with one sweep of his sword, knocked Jonathan's helmet and plume to the ground. A group of Philistines closed in before the Hebrews could rescue Jonathan.

Saul saw the Philistines hack Jonathan to death.

"Jonathan . . .

"Jonathan . . .

"My son, Jonathan!"

And Saul gave a wail that was like the soul escaping from the body.

Gathering every last strength, Saul rose to his feet. He took Arad in his arms and kissed him. Then he unsheathed his sword and handed it to Arad. "Run me through."

Tears streamed down Arad's cheeks. "My Lord . . . I cannot."

Saul took the sword from Arad's hand, put its blade between the armor plates, and, with a gasp, fell upon it, driving its blade deep into his body.

Arad looked at the lifeless body of the King, the body of the man he had cared for. He took the hilt of the sword from Saul's hand and wrenched the blade, dripping with blood, out of Saul's body. He turned it on himself and, with a thrust, mingled his blood with Saul's. He fell, dying, his body strewn across the body of the King.

EIGHT

Absalom thought about God. High on a hill above the valley of the Jabbok, marching toward Mahanaim, Absalom had seen the huge dust cloud of David's fleeing troops, headed north. Where to? Would they lose themselves in the wilderness of Bashan, to be decimated by barbarian tribes?

He felt a moment of sadness about the end of so great a king. But mostly he thought about God. God's Will was clearly evident to Absalom, high on those Gilead hills under the embracing sky. Absalom was chosen. Even in his triumphant entry into Jerusalem, Absalom had not had such an overpowering sense of his destiny. But now David had been vanquished without a sword being raised, and the last question of his forthcoming reign had been answered. God had spoken.

All Absalom's conspiring, his negotiations with elders of the tribes, his passionate leadership, and the inspiration of his very presence, so carefully cultivated in dress and stance —all those years of effort were now culminated with the favor of God.

In a flash of awareness, Absalom was acutely conscious of that favor's terrible burden. What was greatly given could be greatly taken away in a sight as awesome as the dust cloud of David's fleeing troops. If it could happen to David, it could happen to Absalom.

Absalom had seen the furrows on David's forehead, the tension around the eyes, the sudden flashes of petulance and anger. He had wondered as a youth how someone who held so great a power as David could feel such unease. He remembered asking his father, regal in the throne room, what bothered him. David had raised a weary hand and pointed it over his left shoulder. "The Lord is right behind me . . . watching."

The thought had struck young Absalom as bizarre. He could see no fiery God behind his father. But now, suddenly, Absalom seemed to feel a great hand clamped on his shoulder. A power to guide him. A power to crush him. Was this what David had lived with for twenty-five years?

Through Absalom's hatred of his father now seeped a sympathy which he had not known was there. He had felt awe for his father, yes, as he would feel awe for a frowning mountain. Early in his life he had even felt love, and had tried to express it as best he could before it had finally curdled into rage. But he had never felt any outreaching empathy. David the King was a thing unto himself, immune and heedless of the touch of human understanding.

But now he thought of that old man, hateful as he was, trudging along with his remnant of troops, seeking some haven in the hostile wilderness, condemned to wander like Moses in search of some new promised land. This . . . after the grandeur of Jerusalem!

Was God asking of him mercy as well as power? Should he not send fast couriers to David in flight and plead with him to halt? They could talk, as Hushai had suggested. Now that David was lost in defeat, could there not be some way that David could be kept among his own people, first among the elders? Wasn't he tired of power? Wouldn't he be ready to give his counsel to his own son and let the power pass out of his hands?

Absalom could imagine David ensconced with honor at

170

Bethlehem or Hebron to live out his old age where he had lived his youth—in the Judean hills. He could celebrate God with his harp and not be wearied by the clamp of responsibility on his shoulder. Once the rivalry between father and son had been settled and God's favor had passed, could there not be peace between them?

Responsibility had made David fierce and wily. But perhaps age would mellow him. Absalom could see himself, as the years of his kingship went by, coming with his royal retinue to Bethlehem to counsel with his father. They would meet, eye to eye, and Absalom would embrace him. They would sit under the big tree near Jesse's house, eat cheese and figs, drink wine, and watch the sun glowing golden as it settled into the Great Sea. David would tell stories of his reign—stories of conspiracy, intrigue, embattlement, and victory—stories that Absalom would now understand in all their complexities—and he would glean wisdom from the old man. And the old man would cross to Sheol in peace.

Perhaps Hushai was right. Perhaps it would be best to talk.

But Amasa was close at his side, and Amasa was adamant. "When you first entered Jerusalem, Ahithophel gave you sound counsel. Pursue David while he was weak and disorganized and destroy him. But you didn't follow that counsel and David had a chance to cross the Jordan and regroup at Mahanaim. But we are strong now. He must know how strong we are, or he would not run again. He is running now, because he is weak and vulnerable. This time, he must be destroyed. You will never sleep a peaceful night until he is destroyed."

Absalom considered the matter. "Tell me, Amasa, how much do you think he knows of us?"

"Enough to fear us."

"Do you think he has spies in Jerusalem?"

"Oh, I'm sure he hears old women's tales."

"But our strategy? Our strength in numbers, our weakness of too many tribal commands?"

171

Amasa flared. "Who would know our strategy? You. Me. Hushai. And the tribal commanders, all loyal to yourself."

"I know." Absalom looked at the dust cloud. "Still, it is strange, this headlong flight to the north. I would have thought that David would try to defend Mahanaim, or would fall back with the Ammonites. He has friends among the Ammonites. But what is there in Bashan, except wild animals? Still, his forces escaped Mahanaim before we attacked from the north. Suspicious timing."

"Nothing suspicious about it. They have panicked." Amasa pointed to the dust cloud. "Look at that motley uproar! It howls with fear. It slavers with weakness." Amasa's voice grew stentorian. "I pray you, my Lord, let us kill the beast!"

"Can we catch it?"

"Like a wolf pack after a stag. Of course we can catch it!"

Absalom rubbed his chin. "My father's troops are accustomed to move swiftly, as one body. Our troops come from many tribes. They are many bodies who have come together just recently."

"But I have general command. I can hasten them."

Absalom called a council of the tribal commanders and Hushai. He put the question to them. Attack Mahanaim, or pursue David's troops? All the commanders agreed. Pursue David's troops, and capture the King. Only Hushai dissented. In a low voice to which no one paid any particular attention, Hushai asked, "Has not anyone heard of the Forest of Ephraim?"

From his own distant hill, Joab saw the forces of Absalom wheel away from the road to Mahanaim, and start north toward the dust cloud that Joab had carefully stirred up. He turned to Abishai and smiled.

David sat in a house at Mahanaim and grieved for his son. David had wanted to go into battle at the head of his

172

troops, the better to protect Absalom if he were found and captured. But Joab and Abishai would not hear of it. "If the battle goes hard and half of us are killed, so be it. The other half will live to fight another day. But you are King. If you are killed it is over for all of us. You stay here in Mahanaim with the reserves. We will take care of Absalom's army."

David knew the sense of what they said, and though it galled him, he agreed. How could he say that he wanted to go into battle to protect the head of the enemy? But at least he could say, "Deal gently with the young man Absalom, for my sake."

Joab and Abishai had given their assent, but he feared the watchful look on their faces. Those two commanders, he knew, were ingenious at making accidents happen. Therefore, as the troops assembled in Mahanaim before the march, David gave them his blessing, and in the hearing of all ordered again that Absalom be spared. The troops received this command in a sullen silence. But he was still, to them, the King. He prayed that the force of his command still held, regardless of how contrary it was to those warrior minds.

Still . . . he grieved.

Hushai marched with Absalom. His feet felt weighted, but he marched. He would follow this agony through, if need be, to the end, but he hoped to avert the final death-throes by some ingenuity of statecraft. He watched the young man near him, as handsome as David but with a curl of cruelty around the lips. This young man, so forceful, so intelligent, so plagued by the need for recognition and power, might one day make a great king. But now, Hushai determined, he could only bring disaster to all the tribes of Jacob. His venom and anger would tear at the flesh of the nation like the claws of a hawk.

That was why Hushai had done his part to see that David had a better chance of victory . . . if it came to battle. But Hushai had no taste for this battle. He knew as well as anyone the military guiles of David and Joab. This "headlong retreat" that so stirred the confidence of Amasa and the tribal commanders was one of David's ways of choosing his own battle ground, and Hushai cringed at the butchery that could take place in the Forest of Ephraim. It would scar Israel for a generation. He despaired of making Absalom understand, but perhaps through the tribal elders . . . or some before-the-battle anxieties . . . he might be able to make some persuasive inroad into the suicidal determination that now seemed to possess both Amasa and Absalom. So he marched, his legs aching with the weariness of age. He hoped for one last service to Israel, the throne, and the Lord.

The main body of Absalom's troops straggled up the shoulder of a hill as the sun, settling in the west, cast amber rays on its crest. Across a sweep of valley, Absalom and Amasa could see the dust of David's troops and the gleam of their armor set against the dark line of trees that were the edge of the Forest of Ephraim. Amasa was straining to attack, but the march of his slow-moving troops would have been long, and nightfall was coming. Better to wait for morning, when the even slower-moving contingents could catch up. Or perhaps they would just camp along the way as their spirit and available water allowed them. Some troops of Simeon's were having trouble with their pack animals. A commander of the Asherites was in a sulk from some fancied slight, and announced that he would move his troops only in their own good time. A column of Benjamites had decided the victory was won and had gone home to their farms and herds. The Zebulunites, whom Absalom had counted among the most loyal of the northern tribes, were restive about getting back to their harvest. And the men of Judah feared a Philistine attack while they were on some strange compaign in the northern wildernesses of Bashan.

174

Amasa knew that if David and his troops were not soon destroyed, Absalom's army would fall apart. Absalom and Amasa would be at David's mercy. But for that night, at least, he could do nothing, except keep watch on David's troops in the waning light.

He thought momentarily that David might plan a night attack—in his prime he had been fully capable of such a challenge—but he thought David too old and his troops too demoralized for such a maneuver. Still, he chose his night patrols carefully.

Darkness came and the night began its slow progress. No message was received from the troops of Simeon or the Asherites. The Zebulunites kept to themselves, some distance away from the main encampment. Amasa and Hushai sat around a pallid campfire while Absalom paced the ground before it, his hand gripping his sword hilt. Overhead a night-bird cried, a wild lonely sound, repeated again and again.

Hushai prayed the Lord for something to say, but he could think of nothing in the tension of the darkness. It was Absalom who finally spoke. "Amasa, do you think the Zebulunites will fight?"

"They are under my command. Of course they will fight."

Absalom glanced in the direction of the separate Zebulunite encampment. "They are acting strangely."

"They are worried about their crops."

Absalom snorted. "Their crops will not be ripened till the next moon."

"They fear a long campaign."

Absalom's eyes flashed in the firelight. "They have sworn loyalty to me! They were among the first. Even when I was at Geshur, they gave a pledge!"

Hushai sighed. "Loyalty, like wet leather, stretches only just so far."

"But my father . . . David's troops . . ."

"They have been with him for a long time."

"But now . . ."Amasa said, "they crumble."

175

"It may not be as it appears," said Hushai.

Absalom stopped pacing and looked at Hushai. "Say your thought."

"Dust clouds can signal rout. They can also hide disciplined marching troops."

Amasa cut in. "It *is* a rout!"

Absalom held up his hand. "Let him say his thought, Amasa."

"But if it is not?" Hushai rallied all his fading energies. "And if the Zebulunites do not fight. And if the Asherites do not appear. And if the mules lead the troops of Simeon into the Jabbok, what then?" Hushai got to his feet. "I pray you, my Lord, nothing is lost by simple talk. For a sundered Israel, let us parley. It may be that they fear us as deeply as we, perhaps, should fear them. And the Lord may visit us both for His people."

Absalom's hand still raised, Amasa kept his silence.

Absalom started pacing again, his eyes brooding on the ground before his feet. Twigs in the fire crackled. The nightbird cried again. Amasa and Hushai followed Absalom's every movement as he stalked back and forth in the darkness.

Hushai prayed. And he thought about a slender reed named Solomon.

The guards dragged the girl into the light of the fire and flung her on the ground in front of Absalom. She lay there, moaning and quivering. The captain of the guard reported to Absalom. "She went from Jerusalem to En-rogel, the Dragon's Spring. She took messages from Zadok to his son, Ahimaaz. That is how David learned our strategy."

Absalom glared at the captain. "But Zadok did not know our strategy."

Joab sat in his tent, poring over a map of the Forest of

176

Ephraim that he had ordered made many years before. The tent-flap opened and two of the night patrol entered, holding between them a young girl, clad only in a few rags, her hair disheveled, her face smeared with dusty grime. In her hand was a heavy-laden sack of coarse linen, dark-stained at the bottom.

One of the guards reported to Joab. "We found her, my Lord, close to the lines. She asked to be taken to you."

"Release her," Joab said.

She stood, trembling, her head bowed. Joab noticed bruises on her legs and arms. "Where did you come from?" he asked.

"The camp . . ." She stammered to get the words out. "The camp of Absalom."

"What did you bring me?"

She handed him the sack and a scrap of papyrus. Joab read the scrawl on the papyrus. "I HAVE COME TO PARLEY."

Joab opened the sack and pulled out the severed head of Hushai. The tongue was torn out of the mouth. He put it on the floor of the tent beside the map of the Forest of Ephraim.

The guard asked, "Shall we take it to Mahanaim . . . to the King?"

Joab shook his head. "No. The King must not know of this. He is burdened already. Leave it here. Take the girl, and clothe her and see that she is cared for."

The guards bowed and left with the girl.

Alone in his tent, Joab stared at the head of Hushai, the face he had known for years. He wished that Absalom had never been born. He vowed that Absalom would not live another day.

A hot desert wind swept through Mahanaim. David lay on a pallet beside Bathsheba and tried to sleep. But he could not. He could hear the low voices of the night watch outside the window lattice, the scuffle of mule hooves and the occasional bleat of a sheep.

David thought about Absalom. But the image he saw was a six-year-old youngster at Hebron, where David had been King of Judah while Ishbosheth was King of Israel . . . those sweet simple days when all he had had to worry about were the Philistines and the Amalekites. More properly, he let the Philistines and Amalekites worry about him. David, for the last time in his life, had had time. And he had spent some of it with Absalom. Not so much as he spent with Amnon. But some. Absalom would quiver with excitement at the attention.

Even then, his hair was lustrous, his stance princely, and his eyes predatory. If Amnon took attention as his due, Absalom grasped every shred of the time his father gave to him as if it were prey. When he held David's hand, his fingers were tight around David's palm. When David walked, he ran to be beside him. When David taught Absalom the sling, his muscles were bowstring-tight in the effort of learning, his childish face contorted with concentration. Even then, David remembered, Absalom seemed driven.

What a prince he might have been! What a king he might have become! Now, sleepless in Mahanaim, David wondered at the time he had lavished on obscure campaigns in the Judean wilderness, the time he had spent haggling with tribal elders, the hours he had sat in judgment on irate merchants, wailing farmers, and errant families. He had been so profligate with the time he had spent on the needs of kingship. And all the time, Absalom had been growing to maturity, driven by furies of which David was not aware until the murder of Amnon.

But wasn't succession one of the needs of kingship? What time was he spending now to try to cope with a corruption of succession that might have been averted by time spent years before to guide Absalom's youth? David-the-King had been betrayed by David-the-father.

Living there, sweating in the hot darkness, David festered

with the treason, and prayed that his son would not be its victim.

Absalom and Amasa stood on the highest point of the hill outside the encampment and strained their eyes in the first faint light of dawn for some sight of David's troops by the Forest of Ephraim. Absalom's rage at Hushai's treason had cooled a little, assuaged by the very sword-stroke that had cut his head from his body. Still, Absalom had been shaken by the knowledge that David and Joab had found out about his closest counsels. He felt himself revealed as if, as a child, he stood before his father's throne and heard his sins recounted.

No! No more! The power had passed. David's hand on his shoulder had long since vanished. His guidance came from God. He would sing, as his father had sung, the praises of the Omnipotent. He would be blessed, as his father had been blessed, in the responding grandeur. He stood now under the arch of heaven, and waited for the light of day.

As the light came, the movement of David's troops was clear. They were breaking camp and moving into the forest. Figure after figure disappeared into the tangle of trees. "They are going into hiding," Absalom said, "like whipped dogs."

"We'll hunt them down."

Absalom squared his shoulders and handed Amasa a length of gold. "Amasa, comb my hair."

Absalom and Amasa, riding on mules, led their troops to the edge of the forest. From the hill of their encampment, the forest had seemed like any other, a dark brow of trees on the crest of a hill. But as they crossed the valley between, and climbed the ridge to the forest, it had grown steadily more sinister. Now, at the forest's edge, they saw trees, gnarled and massive, that seemed to have been there

179

since the Flood. Between the trees were thickets of dense brush and slippery masses of mossy rock that reared up like the backs of giant animals.

Amasa snorted. "David's troops must be desperate to hide in a refuge like this."

"Ripe to be butchered," Absalom said, "if we can find them."

"We'll find them."

Just then, they heard sounds within the forest, shouts and the clanking of armor.

Absalom and Amasa exchanged glances. "The sheep await us," said Absalom and urged his mule forward.

Amasa followed with a strong force of Issacharites, leading all the troops of Absalom into the Forest of Ephraim.

Ahead, through the trees, they could see a tattered remnant of David's force clambering through the underbrush, but as fast as Absalom tried to move his troops forward, David's men moved faster, deeper into the forest. Fear, Absalom concluded, spurred them, and he wondered what dishevelment of demoralized men they would find when they came upon David's main force. He almost pitied the ease of anticipated victory, the end of David's mighty reign.

But still, there was the forest, an enemy more malignant than any Davidic sword. Not just the trees and underbrush, but the terrain itself conspired against him. Its boulders were at least visible. But the potholes and crevasses were covered with the debris of the forest, and unheeding soldiers were constantly falling into them, bruising their bodies and shattering their legs. Absalom's progress through the forest left a wake of casualties. Even Absalom's mule fractured its leg, and he had to call for another mount, a nervous animal, not easily controlled.

Still, they pressed forward, pursuing that bedraggled detachment of David's men that always seemed to elude them in the heavy shade of the trees. Amasa grew restive and worried that David's force was escaping them at the other side of the forest, but Absalom clung to his vision of some pathetic encampment strewn across the forest floor.

The attack came like the vengeance of God. Fueled by the rage of Joab, David's men fell on Absalom's troops with a lethal fury that stunned the Issacharites with its force and broke their formation. With a discipline forged in years of battle, David's soldiers went about their butchery, cutting their way through column after column of straggling soldiers from the tribal levies. They sprang out of crevasses, charged from behind boulders, dropped out of low-hanging tree limbs like demons of the forest, a curse to all men. Absalom saw all that he had wrought begin to totter.

To his right, the Zebulunites were being torn to pieces, and the Asherites were in a chaos of retreat. Absalom knew that Amasa and the men of Judah were somewhere to his left, but he could not see them in the tangle of the forest. Driving his heels into the flank of his skittish mule, he drove it forward to find the troops of Judah, praying they would be standing fast against David's men.

Gathering speed, the mule lurched, and Absalom felt himself thrown into a low-hanging bough. His neck was caught, viselike, in the fork of the limb, his hair entangled in its branches. The mule had fallen into a pothole, leaving Absalom suspended, his feet kicking in the air. No men of Judah came to his rescue. No men of Judah were visible. No men of Judah could hear his cry above the battle.

He clutched at the limb, writhing to free himself, but the more he struggled, the tighter was the limb's grip and he felt a fierce tugging of his hair. Some live thing seemed to wrench it, as he had once wrenched Mephibosheth's hair.

"You men, over there! This is no time to argue about who is the mightiest warrior in the King's army. There are still enemies in this forest, so stay alert," Joab shouted as he strode away toward a group of wounded men.

Just then one of his men came up to him saying he had

urgent news. Gesturing to a particularly ominous group of trees not too far away, he hurriedly said that he had seen Absalom caught by the neck in the limb of an oak tree, unable to move.

"You saw him? Why did you not strike him to the ground then and there? I would have given you ten pieces of silver and a belt."

The man shook his head. "If you put in my hands a thousand pieces of silver, I would not lift a finger against the King's son. You heard the King's orders about Absalom. If I had killed him, David would have known . . . and you would have kept well out of it!"

"That's a lie," said Joab. "Lead me to where Absalom hangs."

The man led Joab through the woods, followed by the commander's armor-bearers, until they came to the big oak. There, pinioned in the narrow crotch of a branch, was Absalom, his legs dangling an arm's length off the ground. Several of David's troops stood around the tree, their spears poised, guarding the captive.

Joab came close, his eyes focused on Absalom's face and his long hair, tangled in the foliage. Absalom's hands were holding the branch on either side of his neck, struggling to free himself with gasps of effort. Between gasps, he cried, "Let me down! I am the King's son!"

Then Absalom saw Joab. His cry grew more plaintive. "Take me down. Take me to the King." But he looked in Joab's eyes and his body went limp. "No . . . No . . ."

Joab picked up three stout sticks and drove them against Absalom's chest as he was held fast to the tree, still alive.

Joab's and Absalom's eyes met for the last time, but neither man said a word. Then Joab's armor-bearers closed in with their spears, making thrust after thrust into Absalom's body. In his death throes, Absalom screamed, "David . . . David . . . be with me!"

Joab ordered the trumpet sounded, and the slaughter in the forest ended.

182

They took Absalom's body down from the tree and threw it in a pothole in the forest. Joab's armor-bearers piled stones on it until the body was covered, and the pothole was filled to even ground so it would never be found.

Amasa and Absalom's troops fled the forest and went to their homes.

Ahimaaz, son of Zadok the high priest, came to Joab. "Let me run and take the news to the King about the victory."

Joab's face was grim. "This is no day for you to be the bearer of news. Another day you may have news to carry, but not today."

"Listen, my Lord, I risked my life as David's courier. My father risked his life to get the information to me. I have a right . . ."

"The King's son is dead. You want to bear that news, too?" Joab turned away and summoned a Cushite. He told the young man to run to Mahanaim and tell the King what he had seen. The Cushite bowed low before Joab and set off running.

But Ahimaaz pleaded again with Joab. "Let me run after the Cushite. We'll both bring him the news of victory."

"Absalom is dead. The King won't count it any victory. And you won't get any reward for telling him."

"But it *is* a victory, and we risked for it!"

Joab snorted in disgust. "You know that. I know that. But all the King will know is that Absalom is dead."

"Let me go, anyway."

"All right. Go."

Ahimaaz set off running and soon outstripped the Cushite on the road to Mahanaim. An exultation buoyed him along, faster and faster. Once out of Joab's baleful gaze, Ahimaaz could discount what the commander had said. No, it could not be that the King would be so heedless of a victory so dearly won! And over such an enemy!

It had been Ahimaaz who had cared for the servant girl the night before, after she had brought the head of Hushai to Joab. He and his father had been the only ones who had known of her existence before she was captured. Yet she had been the linkage—the crucial linkage between Zadok in Jerusalem and David in the field. And then, just before victory, she had fallen into Absalom's hands.

He had wrapped his cloak around her, given her wine to drink, washed her feet and the grime from her face. And all the while she had cried—not great sobs but a low wail of desolation, a thin, lost sound in the night as persistent as the coming of death. He had tried to comfort her and she had clung to him. But no human warmth could seem to assuage the memory of what had happened to her in Absalom's camp.

He had dared not ask about it for the wrenching it might cause her, but the quivering body in his arms was enough to bring images of Absalom's cruelty to his imagination. What he could do to that young girl, he could do to anyone, and Ahimaaz envied Hushai so quick a death. The girl would have to live with her memory.

He had seen Absalom's body as they had taken it down from the tree, twisted and drenched with blood. But no pity had stirred within him. He saw a serpent, sundered, and felt a sweet relief.

Now he ran, his feet pounding, his lungs straining for air, toward Mahanaim.

David sat between the two gates of Mahanaim with Ira, his priest, and stared out over the tawny hill country to the north of the town. He knew that either messenger or troops would come that way from the Forest of Ephraim, but he didn't know whose messenger, or what troops.

He sighed. "Perhaps it is the fate of old men just to wait."

184

"When you grow old, my Lord, then you may talk about it."

"When you have a back like mine, Ira, you grow old very fast." David ruminated for a few moments. "Ira . . ."

"Yes, my Lord?"

"Do you think Absalom will make a good king?"

"I do not know, my Lord."

David spoke with wistful puzzlement. "I don't know, either. It occurs to me that I don't know that young man at all. He must be kept alive. I must get to know him. There are things I can teach him."

"I am sure."

David's voice saddened. "If he is willing to learn."

"Perhaps . . . once this storm has passed . . ."

"Yes . . . Yes . . . Then."

Ira caught the eagerness in David's voice, the pathos of a tormented father, and he wondered about Absalom. Did he feel an eagerness, too? And where in this was God's Will? Ira had had no qualm or question. David had been the Lord's anointed even from the time of Samuel. By serving David, Ira served the Lord.

Nor did he have any question that the man, David, was a worthy vessel of the Lord's Will. David was a man of titanic accomplishment, the greatest of Israel and the scourge of its enemies. A lesser man would have assumed a greater facade. But David remained a man of wit and frailty and wore his body with as great an ease as he wore his armor. His very self was a testament to the Lord.

So simple not to think further. The Lord's Will was in the hands of Joab, and through Joab the Lord would spill blood for the sake of His anointed. Such was Ira's faith.

But there was David, sitting beside him, tormented. And somewhere in the Forest of Ephraim was Absalom, tormented. Each had come along roads of love, and hate, and anger, and misunderstanding, and attempted reconciliation, and rejection, to this fierce day when the issue

185

might be settled, not by father and son, but by Joab and Amasa. Was this truly the Lord's Will? Did He truly proclaim, for the wonderment of His people, this sorry history?

Ira's faith wavered.

David rose from his seat as he saw Ahimaaz running toward him. Gasping for breath, Ahimaaz bowed low before the King. "All . . . is well."

"What has happened?"

"The Israelites are scattered. We have brought victory to you."

David stepped forward and grasped Ahimaaz's tunic. "How is it with Absalom?"

"Absalom? He is defeated."

Tightening his grasp on the tunic, David looked at Ahimaaz with hawk eyes, and Ahimaaz felt a sinking fear. "Is my son alive?"

"I saw a great commotion," Ahimaaz stammered. "But I do not know what happened."

David stepped back, his hand trembling. "Thank you," he murmured, "thank you for bringing me the news of victory."

Ahimaaz bowed again. "We did it for the greatness of our King." And he retired, shaking.

When the Cushite came to David, the King asked him the same question. "How is it with Absalom?"

The Cushite looked puzzled, but he spoke in a flourish. "May all the King's enemies and all rebels who would do you harm be as that young man is."

David shouted at the Cushite. "IS HE ALIVE OR IS HE DEAD?"

"He is dead, my Lord."

David swayed on his feet and held Ira's shoulder to steady himself. Then he started to walk to his quarters. Ira made a gesture to follow him, but David motioned him back. Step by trancelike step, David went to his quarters and shut the door against the world. Alone, he fell to his knees, wracked with anguish. "O, Absalom, my son, my son!"

Ira was at the town gate when Joab returned with the troops. He drew Joab aside. "The King has been told of Absalom's death. He suffers greatly."

Joab glowered. "He would suffer more if that young monster were still alive."

"Still . . ."

"Where is he now?"

"In his quarters, mourning."

"But we are victorious!"

"His son is dead."

"He should be here at the gate to show his gratitude!"

"I doubt if he will show himself."

Joab was grim. "I will talk to him." And he led the troops through the gate. Noticing that David was nowhere to be seen, they marched silently, almost as if they were an army in defeat.

Joab went straight to David's quarters. He found the King lying on his pallet in a darkened room, his hair disheveled, his face streaked with tears.

Joab kept himself under rigid control, fighting the ache of fatigue. "Your troops have returned, my Lord, with victory. They await sight of you, and your blessing."

David said nothing for a long moment. Then: "What happened with Absalom?"

"He was captured, and killed."

"Who killed him? I will order that man executed."

Joab squared his shoulders. "I killed him."

David reared up off the pallet with an animal growl and grabbed his sword. "Then I will execute you myself!"

David lurched toward Joab, the sword held in both his

187

hands. Joab feinted and wrenched the sword away from David, pushing the King into a chair. Now, you listen to me!"

"Get out! Get out of my sight! You will die for this!"

"You will hear me first."

"No!" David tried to get up from the chair, but Joab held him fast.

"Listen! You have put to shame this day all your servants who have saved you and your sons and daughters, your wives and your concubines."

"Absalom is dead."

"Yes, you love those that hate you and hate those that love you."

"You killed him."

"Yes, and if Absalom were alive and all the rest of us dead, you'd be happy, wouldn't you?"

"I would I were dead myself!"

"You are alive. Now go and show yourself to your troops, or I swear by the Lord that not a man will still be here by nightfall."

David sat motionless.

Joab barked the command. "Go! Now!"

Slowly David rose to his feet.

"Stay, a moment," Joab said. He straightened David's robe, ran his hand through David's hair to straighten it, and dipping a linen in a water bowl, rinsed David's face.

"Now. We go," said Joab.

NINE

D avid could not sleep. He was too old and too wise to trust any victory. All he sensed was the bitter weight of kingship, made more burdensome by loneliness.

They had all come back to him. The men of Judah. The men of Israel. Even Shimei, the crazy Benjamite, had met him on his way back to Jerusalem, groveling. But whom could he trust, now? Whom could he believe? They had followed Absalom. What new usurper would sound a trumpet? Who would his followers be? Even now he heard rumblings of disaffection, and the men of Judah and Israel were exchanging angry words, again—this time over the possession of the King they had dispossessed! He was too fatigued even to appreciate the irony. He felt punished by God, to reign over so fractious a people. He longed for the serenity of the Judean hills.

He stalked past guards posted by flickering lamps in the corridors. He thought of ordering one of them to go and wake up Ira to keep him company, but then thought better of it. Ira needed his sleep. And he was having enough trouble with God without listening to a lot of priestly platitudes. Still, as he thought about it, it seemed as if Ira was the only friend he had left. The loneliness swept over him again.

189

Why had he not just let go? He would have found friends and warmth and kin in Bethlehem. They would have sustained him as the years settled in his bones. He could have let the burden pass to Absalom's shoulders and found solace in the sunlit cycle of the seasons. He would have come back to his youth, and now that youth seemed very precious to him.

But Absalom?

He had heard about what had happened to Hushai from Abishai after David had exiled Joab from his sight, and it had chilled him, even in his grief over Absalom. The news was all the more disturbing because he could envision himself doing such a deed in his early years. A spy was a spy, cut off from the grace of God and man, flesh to be hacked for the glory of God, and for the salvation of His people.

Yet as he thought of what Absalom had perpetrated, he wondered at its concise cruelty. This was no explosion of righteous rage, but a considered use of atrocity. Absalom had spoken in agony and blood. David knew the language. Now he detested it. Could he have unleashed on Israel and Judah so adept a pupil? Could such a man have built the Temple?

David walked into the deserted audience room, illumined by only a few night-lamps. Ahead of him, shadowed and foreboding, was Saul's big chair. It no longer seemed to belong to him. Absalom, he was sure, had sat in it, and received pledges of loyalty from those who now gave their penance to David. But as he wandered about the room, feeling alien, memory kept stabbing at him. Hushai seemed almost a physical presence, sedate and circumspect, stroking his gray-flecked beard and staring at some distant spot with ruminative eyes. Where would he find the wisdom of another Hushai?

He turned to the other side of Saul's big chair and felt the presence of Joab as he had stood there time and again, gnarled and hard as an oak. His eyes had been as shrewd as Hushai's had been mellow. His counsel had been as

190

acerbic as Hushai's had been conciliatory. But no sword had brought Joab's destruction. In a fit of rage over Absalom's death, David had driven him from command, and then, as a sop to the men of Judah (a brilliant piece of statecraft, he had thought at the time), had given the command to Amasa.

But what had he accomplished? His best friend and best commander was gone, and David was left with the pompous incompetence of Amasa, a true peril to the military safety of Israel and Judah.

Still, Joab had given himself to headstrong rage before, and made a travesty of royal will. After the death of Saul and Jonathan at Gilboa, Abner, Saul's commander-in-chief, had set Ishbosheth up as King of Israel while David became King of Judah. For David, this had been an amiable development. He had an affection for Saul's son, his old tent-mate, a wry and peaceable soul who detested war. David anticipated that relations between Judah and the northern tribes would be tranquil. But he had not reckoned on Abner and Joab. Those two choleric men started feuding and skirmishing from the very beginning of David and Ishbosheth's reign. Abner killed Asahel, one of Joab's brothers. In revenge, Joab killed Abner, the bulwark of Ishbosheth's power, who had been talking peace with David. Then the bloodthirsty Rechab and Baanah, hoping to win David's favor, had assassinated Ishbosheth and brought his severed head to David at Hebron. David had been almost as desolate then as he now was at the death of Absalom. He ached at the price he paid for Joab's temper and was determined to pay no such price again.

The desolation he felt was pervasive. Where was Michal? He had gone to her chambers shortly after he had returned to the House of Cedar, hoping that perhaps some reconciliation might take place between them. But a maidservant had told him that she had fled even before Absalom had entered the city. Where had she gone? The maidservant could only tell him that she had gone off with some beg-

191

gar. David had smiled ruefully at that; Paltiel had a farmer's guile. It would have been simple enough for David to have ordered a detachment sent to Ephraim to bring her back, but to what purpose? Just to renew the bitterness between them? Let her stay with Paltiel.

David sat down on the throne and picked up his harp, resting, as it had in the past, by the side of the throne. He wondered who had put it back. Some servant, probably. Perhaps Bathsheba. Or possibly Mephibosheth.

David ran his fingers over the strings, filling the room with ghostly sound, and thought about Mephibosheth. His thoughts were jagged with disquiet. He had been so numbed when Ziba had come to him on Olivet that he had barely been able to hear, let alone assimilate his report that Mephibosheth was staying in Jerusalem to proclaim himself, as the line of Saul, King. In the welter of rebellion, how many kings might be proclaimed? He'd felt only the wrench of Mephibosheth's ingratitude and a further distance from the sacred memory of Jonathan. His action—stripping Mephibosheth of all the lands he had inherited from Saul and giving them to Ziba—had been a heedless reflex. Ziba was loyal; Mephibosheth was not. And it was kingly to reward loyalty.

In later thought, David had found Ziba's story strange. With Absalom come to Jerusalem, bringing with him troops from Dan to Beersheba, did Mephibosheth really think he could make a claim to kingship prevail? David knew that Absalom would have cut him down with all the venom he had vented on Hushai. No crippled rival could have survived Absalom's vaunting will.

But Mephibosheth was alive. He had come, riding on a mule, to meet David on his way to Jerusalem. His feet were not dressed, his hair combed, or his clothes washed. But he was alive, and his face was the face of Jonathan. When David asked him why he had not come with him, Mephibosheth said he feared what Ziba had said. David had not known whom to believe. He decided the estates should be split between Mephibosheth and Ziba. But Mephibosheth had been blithe. "Let him have it all, as long as I have your favor." David had been moved. But even now he wondered if Mephibosheth had made some pact with Absalom to decorate his reign as a courtier from the line of Saul if Absalom would spare his life. He recoiled at the thought, but it festered in his mind. He had guarded Jonathan's seed. Had Jonathan's seed betrayed him? After Absalom he could believe anything. He would drink his cup of gall to the last.

He summoned one of the guards. "Go and wake one of my concubines and bring her to me."

When the concubine came, dressed scantily and trying to make her sleepy eyes seductive, David froze her with a look. "Were you here during the time that Absalom occupied the House of Cedar?"

"Yes, my Lord."

"Was Mephibosheth here?"

"Yes, my Lord. He stayed in his quarters."

"Did he have concourse with the prince?"

The concubine shook her head violently. "The prince visited him once. I do not know what happened. But Mephibosheth hid in his rooms. He did not look at the light of day. We brought him food, but he did not eat. We tried to wash him, but he turned us away. We brought him clean linen, but he would not wear it. He stayed in his quarters, moaning and crying out for you. If you had not returned, I think he would have died.'

David was silent. His finger plucked the strings of the harp, one by one. Finally he said, "Go and wake Mephibosheth. Dress him in his finest linen. Comb his hair and beard. And bring him to me."

Mephibosheth entered the audience chamber with slow steps. He seemed almost a shadow come to life as he moved toward the throne and bowed to the King. "I have heard your music, my Lord. I wondered if I would ever hear its balm again."

David shrugged, his hand resting on his harp. "Our fortune rests with God."

Mephibosheth shuddered. "God has been merciful to Israel."

David looked at Mephibosheth sharply, feeling the air, the room, even the chair he sat upon, grow sinister with Absalom's spirit. But he could not bring himself to probe Mephibosheth's memory and uncover some new revelation about Absalom. Let him find what rest he could in Sheol.

David gestured to Mephibosheth. "Draw near."

Mephibosheth stepped forward. David sensed the presence of Jonathan in great waves, and the awareness was a visceral ache. He spoke in measured words. "It is at a time like this that trust drains. The figures around me seem ghostlike. I cannot see their eyes. I do not know what they think, what curse may be on their lips. I do not know what they hold in their hands. A sword, perhaps. A dagger? I cannot hear them murmur among themselves or know what they conspire. What leading do they have from the Lord, and has He shut His sight from me? I think these things in the night, and carry my night vision into day. It plagues my judgment, Mephibosheth, even with you. I mistrusted you, and I was wrong. Accept the King's apology to the seed of Jonathan. It would have been a death to me if the covenant had been broken."

Mephibosheth stood before David, his head bowed. When he raised his head, David saw tears. He spoke softly. "I will dance before the King."

David hesitated. Then he put his harp to his shoulder and his fingers plucked the strings. With a precarious grace, Mephibosheth moved to the rhythms of the music, balancing on his twisted feet, his arms held out from his shoulders to steady himself on thin air. His smile was seraphic as his head moved to the beat of the music.

David felt transported in memory. Images swirled around the dancing figure in a celebrant evocation. David was exulant in song.

Praise Him with the sound of the trumpet:
  praise Him with psaltery and harp.
Praise Him with the timbrel and dance:
  praise Him with stringed instruments and organs.
Praise Him upon loud cymbals:
  praise Him upon the high sounding symbols
Let everything that hath breath praise the Lord!

Suddenly Mephibosheth lost his balance. He stumbled,
lurched forward, and crumpled before the throne. David sat
there and looked at that face and he knew that the covenant
was strong as the knit of the souls of David and Jonathan.

Twenty-five years after the death of Saul and Jonathan,
David sat in the nighttime quiet of the audience chamber
of the House of Cedar. Mephibosheth was sitting on the
floor next to the throne, his head resting on David's knee.
As he had, time after time, in years past and in the privacy
of his solitudes, David played his harp and sang his lament.

The beauty of Israel is slain upon thy high places:
  how are the mighty fallen!
Tell it not in Gath,
  publish it not in the streets of Askelon;
Lest the daughters of the Philistines rejoice,
  lest the daughters of the uncircumcised triumph.
Ye mountains of Gilboa, let there be no dew,
  neither let there be rain, upon you, nor fields of offerings:
For there the shield of the mighty is vilely cast away,
    the shield of Saul, as though he had not been anointed
      with oil.
From the blood of the slain, from the fat of the mighty,
The bow of Jonathan turned not back,
  and the sword of Saul returned not empty.
Saul and Jonathan were lovely and pleasant in their lives,
  and in their death they were not divided:

They were swifter than eagles,
   they were stronger than lions.
Ye daughters of Israel, weep over Saul,
   who clothed you in scarlet, with other delights,
Who put on ornaments of gold upon your apparel.
   How are the mighty fallen in the midst of the battle!
Oh, Jonathan, thou wast slain in thine high places.
   I am distressed for thee, my brother Jonathan:
Very pleasant hast thou been unto me:
   thy love to me was wonderful, passing the love of women.
How are the mighty fallen,
   and the weapons of war perished!

AFTERWORD

AFTERWORD

T he source for the story told in this novel is the Hebrew
Scriptures, First and Second Books of Samuel. I relied
primarily upon *The New English Bible* translation for my
historical facts, and for most of the quotations. The excep-
tions are the selections from the Psalms, and the text of
David's Lament for Saul and Jonathan (II Sam. 1:19–27)
which were taken from the King James Version because of
the magnificence of the language.

For guidance in working through the Biblical text, I used
the *Interpreter's Bible* and the *Interpreter's Dictionary of
the Bible*. I needed guidance. As the *Interpreter's Bible*
points out in the introduction to the books of Samuel, "The
Hebrew text of Samuel shares with that of Ezekiel the doubtful honor of being the most corrupt in the Old Testament,"
and cites instance after instance of "glaring inconsistencies."
In my early readings of the text, I felt hopelessly lost in a
literary Forest of Ephraim. Did David kill Goliath, or did
Elhanan? Did Absalom have a family, or didn't he? Did
Saul take his own life, or was he killed by an Amalekite?

Such puzzles were magnified by the numerous cases where
the books of Samuel give two or more accounts of the same
narrative. There are two different stories of the Ziphite be-

trayal of David to Saul, and David's subsequent sparing of Saul. The first story has David cutting off a piece of Saul's shirttail as the old king went into a cave "to relieve himself" (1 Sam. 23:19–24:22). The other story involves David's removal of Saul's spear and water jar from the royal tent (1 Sam. 26:1–25).

Scripture has its privileges, but a novelist has to choose between the shirttail and the water jar. He cannot have both and maintain a coherent narrative. I made my choices for various reasons, primarily selecting the narrative which I felt best illuminated character and which made the best historical sense. For instance, the story of David and Goliath (I Sam. 17) shows David as the feisty and courageous youth that he certainly must have been, but details such as "He struck Goliath down and gave him a mortal wound, though he had no sword," make one suspect that one is reading a historical whopper. The validity of the tale is further compromised by the statement that "David took Goliath's head and carried it to Jerusalem." This, on quick reading, sounds reasonable enough, until one remembers that in David's youth, Jerusalem was a stronghold of the Jebusites, a non-Hebrew tribe of uncertain origin, and was not captured by the Hebrew forces under David and Joab until some twenty or more years later! (II Sam. 5:6–9)

The other story of the young David's introduction to Saul's court states that David was enlisted as Saul's harp player and that because Saul "loved him dearly" he became the king's armor-bearer (I Sam. 16:14–23). This version also tells something about David's character—his art, his beauty, and his loyalty to the king. It seems to make a lot more sense historically. David and Goliath reeks of myth-making.

But even though the books of Samuel give several different factual versions of the same narrative, they certainly give us fact—lots of facts—usually as crisp and unadorned as a dispatch off a news wire. Consider: "So they set up a tent for Absalom on the roof, and he lay with his father's concubines in the sight of all Israel" (II Sam. 16:22).

A fact—be it a shirttail or a water jar—I could accept. Facts are, after all, the grist of a novelist's mill. And if one set of facts seems less likely than another, so be it. A choice must be made, provided each set of facts is in the text.

The questions start to swarm when the Hebrew scribes explain facts and attribute motivations to actions. We can, for instance, accept what Saul did as legitimate history. But when Scripture—and subsequent Biblical criticism—go on to explain *why* he did it, the reason does not necessarily fit the action. Perhaps because neither scribe nor critic wanted to confront the *real* motivation, the subtext of the story. If so, personal judgment distorts history, and we are left looking at a faulty mirror of the past.

But who can know why a person takes a given action? Honest people—be they judges, theologians, historians, or novelists—can construct scenarios of motivation with varying degrees of plausibility, and each may be arguable. Different times can give us different insights into Scripture, and all may reveal parts of the heritage which is our substance.

This novel can be regarded as an exploration of the homoerotic elements which are, in my judgment, implicit (and sometimes very nearly explicit) in the books of Samuel. It is certainly not the only interpretation that can be made of the text, but I believe it to be the most plausible explanation of the actions of Saul, David, and Jonathan. Given the context of the times in which the books were written, and the force of Hebrew tradition, I believe the scribes went as far as they could in revealing that subtext. Certainly the language used in describing the relationship of David and Jonathan is as erotically romantic as any used in the Bible, except for the Song of Solomon. And the scribes spare few details in describing Saul's jealous rages at David, or his pathetic attempts at reconciliation.

If this homoerotic interpretation of the books of Samuel

201

has been generally ignored or rejected, it does not, in my judgment, reflect on that interpretation's plausibility. Rather, it reflects the homophobia that has permeated Hebrew and Christian thought and distorted our historical perspective.

I wish to express my appreciation to Randall E. Greene, Lucianne Goldberg, Patricia Rummel, Steven Weinstein, and a tribal elder of Old Testament scholarship (who prefers to remain anonymous), for their help in writing this book. I am also indebted to Dr. Tom Horner for his book *Jonathan Loved David* (Westminster Press, 1978), a study of homosexuality in Biblical times.

A final word. When I was first threading my way through the books of Samuel as research for this novel, I turned in my hour of need to the *Interpreter's Bible*. There, heading the roster of editors, was the name of George Arthur Buttrick. My eyes filled. During my teens and early twenties, Dr. Buttrick was my minister and helped guide me through some of the turmoils of my adolescence. Now he helped guide me through a scriptural Forest of Ephraim. I was grateful to him then, and I am grateful to him now.

New York City, 1978

W. H.